STAMPED OUT

A Mail Carrier
Cozy Mystery Series

BOOK ONE

BY
TONYA KAPPES

ACKNOWLEDGMENTS

This book is dedicated to Ashley Yungbluth.
Not only has Ashley become an amazing reader, but she's also become a great friend to me over the years.
When I wanted to write the Mail Carrier Cozy Mystery Series, I knew I could ask Ashley anything I needed since she is a clerk with USPS.
I honestly had no idea how hard they work until I started to pick Ashley's brain. I just knew that some really GREAT mysteries could happen, and what better sleuth than someone in all of our daily lives…a mail carrier.
Thank you, Ashley, for taking the time to answer all my questions and being the wonderful you that you are!

I'd also like to thank Mariah Sinclair for the adorable covers for the Mail Carrier Series. They are so fun and fit my writing style perfectly. You're a genius.

Thank you to Red Adept Editing for the wonderful editing job you do to make my words make sense.

And a huge thank-you to my husband, Eddy. He does all the things that would normally take me away from writing. Without him by my side, I'd not be able to be a full-time writer and fulfill my dream.

ONE

Have you ever been around one of those people who say there's something coming or something about to happen? Or you've been thinking 'bout her and she calls at that moment, that instant?

My best friend, Iris Peabody, she's not one of those psychics or anything, but she does get those weird feelings every once in a while. The first time we were in third grade. She swore to me how she'd seen a vision of Bobby Peters, the cutest boy in school, kissing me on the old rubber tire that was cemented into the ground on the playground. As soon as the teacher said it was time for recess, I darted out to that playground and perched myself right on top of that tire.

Until...

Bobby Peters himself ran by and pushed me right off, sending me to the ground and breaking my wrist. Boy, was Iris wrong.

Then there was another time when we were in high school and Iris told me she'd had one of them visions where Bobby Peters was going to ask me to prom. When I saw him walk over to our table in the cafeteria, my heart went pitter-pat.

Until…

He up and asked Iris. She went.

It wasn't until years later, when I'd already gotten married to Richard Butler—making me Bernadette Butler, stay-at-home mom and ex-United States postal worker— and Iris was already divorced from Bobby Peters when she called me up at three p.m. one afternoon. I was getting ready to head on over to the high school football stadium to watch Grady. Oh no, he didn't play football; he was the Sugar Creek Gap grizzly bear mascot that did get promoted to manager of the team the following year. Still, I went to every game Sugar Creek Gap High School played to watch my boy run up and down the sidelines in the ridiculous bear outfit, waving the high school flag in our very small town of Sugar Creek Gap, Kentucky.

Anyways, back to Iris. Well, she called me right before I was setting out for the game, asking all sorts of questions about Richard and whether I'd talked to him. Her exact words were, "I feel like something is wrong with Richard."

To this day, I still get chills thinking about it.

Iris insisted I call him, but I knew Richard was away on business in our neighboring state of Tennessee, according to the online calendar we shared. There was no reason to bother him, especially when Iris's little "feelings" had never come true yet.

I was cheering on the cute bear when I noticed the state Sheriff had showed up at the game. It was like a slow-motion scene when I recalled seeing them ask someone a question, and the person had pointed directly at me. The Sheriff officers' eyes met mine, and my stomach dropped. Iris Peabody's feeling about my beloved Richard had come true: he had been killed in a car wreck on his way to his meeting.

I'm Bernadette Butler, United States postal carrier. Mom to Grady Butler. Widow.

***

"Good morning, Vince."

Vince Caldwell was sitting outside on one of the many swings across the long covered porch at the Sugar Creek Gap Nursing Home, looking at the morning paper.

My phone rang just as I'd walked up. It was Iris. This was the second time she'd called this morning and the second time I'd sent her to voicemail.

"Mornin', Bernie." Vince pulled the readers off the bridge of his nose and looked up through his bushy gray eyebrows. He patted the open space next to him and put down his crossword puzzle. "I was thinkin' of you this mornin'. About to turn cold. I hope you start dressing warmer. I'd hate for you to catch a chill."

"Thank you. I think about you every morning." I took a seat and at that moment realized exactly why Iris had called me but hadn't left a message.

Earlier I had been running late for my route, and I wanted to try to finish a little early since it was game day.

"I still can't believe it's been ten years." Vince reached over and patted my leg. "We sure still miss Richard and his guitar."

"Yeah. Me too." I sucked in a deep breath. My heart sank into my stomach when I looked at my watch to see the date.

The anniversary of Richard's death. Something I'd never forgotten...until today.

"You and Grady headin' over to the cemetery before the big game?" Vince asked, because it was high school football season, and wouldn't you know, my son Grady had gotten his degree in sports management with a minor in

English and was now Sugar Creek Gap High School's English teacher and head football coach.

"I'm sure we will." I tugged open my mailbag and took out Vince's mail. We probably weren't, but I wasn't going to tell anyone. I usually went to see Richard alone. "You want this or want me to put it in the mailbox?"

It wasn't long after Grady was born that Richard and I had decided I'd be a stay-at-home mom and quit my job as a mail carrier. Childcare was expensive, and Richard had just gotten his first good sales job, which took him out of town a lot. It made more sense for me to quit my job than to try to find somewhere or someone to watch our son.

After Richard had passed, I'd gone back to the post office. They'd offered to give me my route back, which was a driving route, but the downtown-area walking route was available. It was much harder to walk and carry the mail, but staying outdoors kept my mind clear and helped me escape from thinking too much about Richard.

"I'll take it," Vince said, bringing me out of my thoughts. Vince was one of the many elderly citizens who had moved to the retirement condos the nursing home offered. My parents lived here too. They weren't retired by any means, but it was a low-cost and low-maintenance way of living, and they loved it here.

"Well, if I'm going to get to the game on time, I better get hustling." As I stood up, the chains holding up the swing clanked. I handed him his mail.

"Growllll." Vince did his best impression of the grizzly bear sound the football crowd made when someone scored a touchdown. He got up too. "Goooooooo Grizzlies!"

"Rah, rah." I laughed and pumped my fist in the air. I noticed an Uber driver had pulled up. "Where are you going?"

"Emergency city council meeting today. I've heard of some rumblings about Chuck Shilling selling his majority share of the country club to someone. Apparently, at last night's commissioners' meeting, things got a little heated." He didn't mention who might have bought the country club. "From what I understand, Dennis Kuntz is all up in arms. Should be a good one."

"Maybe I'll stop in on my route." I waved him off before I made my way into the building.

Dennis Kuntz and Chuck Shilling owned the one hundred twenty acres the country club sat on, so why would Dennis be so upset?

I pondered the question as I dropped the mailbag to the floor and filled the small community boxes as quickly as possible before I locked them back up and headed out in record time.

In light of the news of the sale of the country club—which was huge if what Vince had told me was true—maybe no one would remember what today meant to me. Not that I didn't love the way my community rallied around me and Grady, but it was as if they rehashed it every year when I was just wanting to grieve on my own.

The bright sun had warmed the autumn day enough that I could take off my sweater. I tied it around my waist and walked over the Old Mill Creek bridge. Once over the bridge, I was standing right where I'd started my morning: next to the post office and across the street from where I'd begin the rest of my morning route. The downtown businesses were on the left side of Main Street.

Eventually, I'd get to the small neighborhoods on the west side of downtown then make my way back to downtown, where I'd deliver all the mail to the business district of Sugar Creek Gap, which included the courthouse, doctors' building, bank, and various other businesses. I liked to finish my day with a few neighborhoods just east of downtown that circled back to the post office.

Briefly, I stopped to listen to the sound of the babbling brook swimming across the rocks as the old mill pushed the water down the creek. It was a daily ritual that I loved, only today there were a lot more cars on the bridge than usual.

When I crossed the street, I noticed the cars were pulling into the courthouse parking lot.

Out of curiosity about what Vince had said about the country club, I decided to switch up my route and deliver the mail to the courthouse just so I could pop my head into that emergency meeting.

Social Knitwork was the first business I came to. It was our local yarn shop, owned by Leotta Goldey. She was a whiz with any sort of material. She was the go-to gal for anything that needed to be altered and lettered and had a monopoly on all things with names on them, including all the business she got from the Sugar Creek Gap schools and sports teams.

When I pushed through the door, the bell above it knocked against the glass. Leotta looked up.

"Morning, Bernadette," she greeted me with a pair of knitting needles in her hand. "You doing all right today?"

"I sure am." I headed over to the counter. I reached around and grabbed her mail out of my bag, putting it in the basket that sat next to the register. "No mail today?"

"Nope." She stood over a customer's shoulder, watching them knit something. I generally was here at the same time each day, which was when Leotta gave lessons as well. I was not a knitter or any type of crafter, but I did enjoy watching. "I'll have some tomorrow. I'll be writing out my bills this afternoon." She pointed one of the needles to a coatrack, where some fluffy knitted fall-colored scarves hung. "I made some new scarves for tonight's game. You take one if you like. It's gonna turn real cold this week."

"These sure are pretty." I thumbed through them. "Grady and Julia gave me the personalized scarf for my birthday this summer that I think you made. I better use it, or they'll tan my hide," I joked, thinking Grady probably had no idea that Julia had given it to me.

"That's right." She looked up at me and smiled from over the student's shoulder. "He's such a good boy, Bernadette. And that Julia. She's a quick learner."

Julia Butler was his wife. They'd met at college. She worked as a secretary for Mac Tabor, a good family friend who was the local architect. She'd graduated from business school. She and Grady had gotten married a couple of years ago and had yet to give me a grandbaby.

"Quick learner?" I asked.

"Yes. She's been coming over here and taking a class from me during her lunch break."

That was news to me, but it didn't seem odd, since Julia's office was just a couple doors down.

"You be careful out there this morning." She pointed her needle toward the window at the street. "All sorts of people cancelled their knitting appointments because they are up in arms about the sale of the country club. Did you hear about last night's meeting?"

"Somebody said something about it over at the nursing home this morning." I watched alongside her as another car zoomed down the street.

"I wonder why so many people care." Leotta shrugged and walked back to her student.

"I have no idea. I'm not a member of the country club." I put my hand on the handle of the door.

"I'll see you at the game," Leotta called out to me from across the shop.

"Sounds good."

My phone buzzed. I stopped on the sidewalk and pulled the cell out of my pants pocket.

When I saw it was Iris for the third time, I figured she really wanted something, so I answered it.

"Hey, Iris," I answered as I continued to deliver the mail of the local businesses. Mostly the owners were busy with customers or not in the fronts of their shops when I delivered their mail, so I'd pop in and out as quickly as I could.

I'd pretty much perfected my system over the last ten years.

"Where have you been? I've been calling and texting all morning. I about left pies in the oven to come find you." Iris sounded a little more on edge than the typical yearly feeling-bad-for-her-friend call.

Maybe she was calling about the pumpkin sugar cookies I'd volunteered us to make for the high school boosters.

"I'm fine. I'll meet you at my house right after I get finished delivering my route." I didn't tell her how I'd already baked several dozen of the pumpkin sugar cookies last night when I couldn't sleep. "I totally forgot it was *the* day until Vince Caldwell reminded me. I feel awful. I bet Grady wonders why I haven't texted him."

"Huh?" Iris sounded all sorts of confused on the other end of the line.

"Richard's date of death." Was she pulling my leg? Iris never forgot.

"Oh my God!" Iris's voice was so loud it made my brain rattle. "Bernadette, I'm so sorry. How are you? Did you get any sleep? You're working? Of course you didn't get any sleep and you just said you were working. I'm a bad friend."

"You're a great friend. I'm fine. I slept," I lied. "I just told you that I totally forgot." I stopped shy of Tranquility Wellness to make sure I didn't disturb any sort of class or clients' quiet time. Tranquility Wellness was a one-stop Zen shop that did all the things the name would suggest, like spa treatments, yoga classes, meditation classes, nutrition classes, and any sort of spa treatments that I wanted to check out.

"So if you weren't calling to check on me so early this morning, then what's up?" I asked.

"First off, I think it's a good sign you forgot. Maybe you can start dating now."

Leave it up to Iris to fix me up. She'd been trying to do so for the past nine years, leaving me one year to grieve.

"Not on your life. The last thing I want is a man to have to cook and clean for." I looked in the window to see if there was a class before I crept in and laid the mail on the counter. "What's up?"

For a brief moment, I stopped and took a deep breath. Even though I knew Peaches Partin, the owner, used a machine to pump a spa smell from a bottle into the vents, it still made me feel good to inhale and exhale the fragrance.

"I had me a feeling. I know you don't want to hear about it, but I was wondering if you've been by Mac Tabor's house yet?"

I'd asked her to stop telling me about her "feelings" after Richard's death.

"No. I haven't gotten that far in my deliveries," I told her. "I'm about to stop at Pie in the Face. You there?"

Iris had created her business, Pie in the Face, after she'd caught Bobby Peters cheating on her in their own bed. Not only were he and the girl all snuggled up, they'd been eating Iris's homemade pie right out of the pie plate.

Forget he was cheating; Iris *never* let anyone eat out of the pie plate.

"You didn't even cut a piece out of the pie plate?" was
what Iris had told me she'd said to the cheating couple
when she found them in bed with her pie plate. "You get a
pie in the face!" she yelled at them as she picked up the pie
and slammed it into his face.

She had come to our house all torn up, but Richard and
I couldn't stop laughing. Richard had suggested she make
her baking side hustle into a real business. That was also
when he had jokingly said she should call it Pie in the Face
so whenever Bobby had to drive downtown to get to his
lumberyard, the name on the bakery would be a constant
reminder of his philandering ways.

She ran with Richard's idea and had a very successful
bakery now.

I did bake some items for her, and she paid me for
them, but most nights, we were still baking in my farm
kitchen, keeping each other company. If not for Iris and our
friendship or our fun nightly baking sessions at my house, I
didn't know what I'd do with all my free evenings now that
Grady was married off.

That was when being a widow was the hardest. Night.

"I'm not at the bakery. I had a few deliveries this
morning, and now I'm off to the high school to help teach

Cake Decorating 101." Iris was also the baking consultant for the high school's home economics department.

"Anyways, when you get to Mac's house or business, make sure he's all right. And I have some outgoing mail, so be sure to grab it, because I'm not sure Geraldine even heard me when I left. She was on her phone Instagramming some of the pies." Geraldine Workman was Iris's only employee.

Iris and I hung up. I quickly texted Grady.

I knew Grady would be too busy in his classroom to even read my text, but I still didn't want the day to go by and Grady think I didn't remember.

A group of men was standing on the sidewalk in front of the Wallflower Diner, my mom and dad's place. One of them was Dennis Kuntz. I walked slower and pretended I was going through the bag to collect the diner's mail.

I recognized the other men from the football games. They all liked to hang over the chain-link fence instead of sitting in the stands with their wives.

"I'm telling you, Mac Tabor threatened me last night when I told him I didn't agree with Chuck selling his part of our country club to him. He's not going to get away with it."

When anyone mentioned Mac's name, it got my attention.

Dennis Kuntz's big belly hung over his pants, and a toothpick stuck in the corner of his mouth. His thin brown hair was combed to the side to help try to cover up the baldness, but he didn't do a good job of it. He had plump cheeks.

"I heard it," I heard one of them say, but I didn't look up to see who it was. "This emergency city council meeting better settle it, because I don't have time to listen to this crap at tonight's game. We've got to bring home a win." The man shook his head. "The city council and the commissioners better get on the same page before this little town implodes."

As the mother of the coach, it was hard to pinch my lips shut. These men loved to give their two cents on how they'd run the plays that Grady gave the boys on the field. Once, I hadn't kept my mouth shut, and Grady had been mad at me for a week. He said I should know better and it was part of being a mom of a coach.

Nonetheless, I was a mom—a Sugar Creek Gap Grizzly mom that was a bear in her own right.

"Mac Tabor and Chuck Shilling will regret it if they show up this morning." Dennis Kuntz folded his hands over his big belly.

If it hadn't been for them talking about Mac and how Iris was hell-bent on those feelings of hers, I would probably have just walked on by with that night's game my only care in the world.

"You only own forty percent of the country from what Chuck Shilling told me last night after football practice it was a done deal."

Another one of the men had spoken up, and I recognized the voice as Peter Dade's. Peter's son, Samuel, was the star of the high school team. I knew his wife, Eileen, from the boosters.

"Chuck pretty much said it was a done deal. Said it right there while we were standing on the fifty-yard line." Another one of the men in the circle had stuffed some money into his wallet and was trying to put it in his back pocket when his elbow hit me. "I'm sorry."

"No problem." I stopped, nearly stumbling over my own feet. "I should've been watching where I was going instead of sorting the mail." I sucked in a deep breath and slid my gaze over to Dennis.

"Ain't you Richard's widow?" Dennis asked me with furrowed brows.

"Yes." It was a title I hated, but it was what it was.

"You got a great son. Good football coach. I'm really looking forward to tonight's big game." He smacked Peter on the back. They all nodded. Well, not Dennis.

"Your husband and Mac Tabor were best friends." Dennis's chin lifted. He stared down his nose at me.

"Yes, they were," I confirmed. My stomach tightened. I could feel the gut punch coming.

"You tell him that if he thinks he's going to get his hands on my country club, he'll have to go through me to do it," Dennis said through gritted teeth.

The other men laughed.

"I'll see you gentlemen tonight." I hurried past them and pushed the diner door open.

"Go, Grizzlies!" My dad sat at the counter with the other regulars.

"Go, Grizzlies." I pumped a fist in the air and weaved in and out among the full tables. "Here's the mail." I handed my mom the stack of various food-service bills and magazines she loved to display throughout the diner for those who were eating alone. "What's the deal with the country club?"

"Sure enough, there was a line out the door when we got here." Mama shook her head.

Her hair was still nice and brown, giving me hope I wouldn't inherit the gray hair my father had gotten in his fifties. Mama was a little plump around the waist and hips from all those years of good cooking for all the people in Sugar Creek Gap. The years had been kind to her. She had very few wrinkles and wore very little makeup.

"You know I can't make hide nor hair of the truth, but I do know something about Mac Tabor," she continued. "I was gonna ask Julia about it this morning, but she grabbed a biscuit and coffee before she headed out. Something about a long day."

Julia and Grady lived in the one-bedroom apartment above the diner. It was perfect for them because it was fairly close to their jobs. Julia's office was a few shops down at Tabor Architects, and the high school was just about a mile down the road. Really, I should have been living in the apartment and they should have had the farm. But I couldn't think about that right now.

"Uh-oh, you got that look in your eye." Mama handed me a Styrofoam box filled with some biscuits. "What are you thinking?"

"Nothing." I shrugged and took the box. "Harriette?" I asked with a nod at the biscuits.

"Yes. She's got the ladies coming over this morning for some front-porch gossip." Mom winked. "I told her I'd send the biscuits with you." Mom always had me delivering food, as if I was Uber Eats or something. "Gertrude has made some of her blueberry jam and canned a lot for the winter. I think I'll get some for the diner."

Gertrude Stone, hands down, made the best jam in Sugar Creek Gap.

"You in a hurry?" Mom asked when I put the container in my mailbag and started to wave.

"Yes. I'm thinking about switching up my route and heading over to the city council meeting to see what's going on around here." I sighed. "It appears as if everyone has lost their minds over this."

"Rightfully so. When changes happen in a community, every one of us is trying to figure out where we will belong in the new system. I think that's what's going on." Mom swiped the towel across the counter before she tucked it back into her apron. She took a to-go bag from underneath the counter. "For Rowena. Tell her they are from Granny."

"Aww." I took the bag of leftovers my mom liked to give my cat. "She'll love it." I stuck it in my bag. "Will I see you tonight?" I asked her.

"Of course you will," she said. Mom and Dad never missed anything of Grady's. Even now in their mid-seventies, they were just as active as the day I'd brought him home from the hospital.

I gave her a quick hug and my dad a kiss before I headed out the door.

Quickly I delivered the mail for the other shops between the diner and Tabor Architects.

"Good morning. I'm so glad to see you," I greeted Julia, my daughter-in-law, when I walked into the front office.

"You won't believe how crazy people have gotten over Dennis Kuntz and his partner, Chuck Shilling, selling the country club." Then Julia told me some news I'd yet to hear. "And how Mac is buying it."

So it was confirmed. This was news that would travel fast in Sugar Creek Gap.

"He is?" I wondered if Iris had had a feeling because she'd heard about the big news.

"Yes. Mac has been doing some layouts for the new condos he wants to build. He told them about his plans at the city council meeting last night. Worst mistake ever." Julia shook her pretty blond hair and put her hand up to her head. "I've already got a throbbing headache from people calling and protesting. What am I to do? I don't make the decisions around here."

About that time, the phone rang. Julia raised a finger to signal me to hold on.

I glanced out the door and noticed a few of the city council members and the mayor walking toward the courthouse with some signs under their arms. I almost got a crick in my neck trying to see what the signs said but couldn't get past their glares at me through the window. What had I done? I shook my head and turned back to my daughter-in-law.

"Tabor Architects," she answered the phone. "I'm sorry. Mr. Tabor isn't in right now. May I take a…" Julia pulled the phone away from her ear and looked at it before replacing it in the cradle. "This town has lost their minds." The phone rang again. She grabbed it but put her hand over the receiver of the phone and mouthed, "I'll save you a seat tonight in the stands."

TWO

Sugar Creek Gap wasn't a tourist town. Our little community had been built on generations of families. We were a small community, but through the years, the owners of big farms had sold off various acres and built several subdivisions.

Sugar Creek Gap was a tiny community surrounded by mountains.

Sugar Creek Gap had been founded as an old mill town since it was nestled in the mountains. The old mill wheel was the first one built, and the preservation committee made sure to keep it running. Though we didn't have any mill operations today, it was still a neat piece of history and was unique to have it right smack-dab in the middle of downtown.

On most fall mornings like this one, you'd find residents who had walked downtown to get a nice cup of hot coffee and sit next to the wheel as they enjoyed the scenery and caught up with friends.

Not this morning. It looked as if everyone had gotten their coffee from the Roasted Bean and headed to the courthouse.

Our courthouse was located right behind the mill wheel and housed all the officially elected offices, clerks' offices, PVA and much more. Most of the lawyers in town even rented office space there. The Sheriff department was in the back, and the volunteer fire department was located in the building next to the back parking lot. It was a one-stop legal shop for all of Sugar Creek Gap.

Even the library's parking lot, which was right next to the courthouse's lot, was full.

I swung my mail carrier bag around me to rest on my back as I tugged open the heavy leaded-glass doors. The hallway was filled with people talking and drinking their coffee. The clerk's office always had a lot of mail and gossip, so I headed there first.

"Hey, Bernadette, you're early." Trudy Evan looked up from behind her computer and smiled. "I guess you heard about last night. Law had to be called and everything."

I laid their rubber-banded mail on the counter and leaned on it.

"Really?" I'd yet to hear that little bit of juicy gossip. "The sheriff?"

"Yep. Angela was getting it when she ran into the courtroom after Mac threatened Dennis Kuntz." Trudy shook her head. "I'm guessing Mac done told you." She eyeballed me.

"You know what, Trudy, I've not talked to Mac. I had no idea he was even trying to buy the country club until Julia told me a minute ago," I told her.

It was unusual for Mac to keep such a big secret from me. Uneasiness pierced my stomach.

"It's not a done deal from what I heard. I think Mac's signing the papers this afternoon." She dragged the mail off the counter and took the rubber band off. She started to thumb through it, sorting it into different piles as she continued to talk. "The mayor and a few of the council members are really trying to stop it. They don't want condos going up, but if you ask me," she looked up and whispered, "the city council members get free membership, and they don't want to lose that perk."

"Anyways, if you want to get a good seat this morning"—she dragged her eyes to the other side of the room and gave a quick nod—"head through that door. You might have to stand, because the courtroom is already filled up. Judge Mason had to call off court just so they could have this emergency meeting." She shook her head. "I feel so sorry for Emmalynn Simpson. She and Kenneth have been through the wringer on this one. Someone said Kenneth is the reason the country club is going to have to file for bankruptcy if they don't sell it."

Murmuring and footsteps from outside the door caught her attention.

"I bet it's about to start." Trudy grabbed a tube of lipstick and put some on. "I heard the TV cameras were going to be here."

TV? I watched Trudy scurry off to the door she'd told me to go through then followed. There wasn't a local television station, so I wasn't sure what she meant, though my curiosity had been piqued.

"Told ya this was a good spot." Trudy folded her arms and leaned back against the wall.

It was standing room only in the courtroom. The judge's bench and the court reporter's desk had been replaced by three tables placed in a U-shape. If I counted correctly, there was a seat with a microphone for every city council member, twelve in all plus one for the mayor.

There was a podium in the middle of the U-shaped tables with a microphone. As the city council members took their seats, I noticed Kenneth and Emmalynn Simpson sitting in the front row of what would be the jurors' box. Dennis Kuntz was next to them.

Mayor Leah Burch walked in and took the middle seat. The city council members all filed in and took seats at the other tables. After everyone appeared to be in their places, Leah stood up.

"As we can all see, the matter of selling the country club has come to everyone's attention. We all know last night's meeting got a little carried away and out of control. Today we've invited members of the country club and the residents of the area to come and give us some insight on how they feel." Leah took a deep breath and looked down at the list.

I glanced around to look for Mac but didn't see him or Chuck Shilling.

"Ashley Williams is not only a council member but someone who does live in the country club neighborhood." Leah looked at Ashley, who had a prestigious spot at one of the tables.

Ashley stood up and adjusted her clothing on her way to the podium to address the crowd.

"I'm Ashley Williams. As you know, I sit on the city council and was appalled to hear the city commissioners held a meeting and approved the new annex for the sale of the country club, giving Chuck Shilling, the majority stakeholder, the ability to sell the club—without the consent of Dennis Kuntz—to Mac Tabor. We have to stand together always if we care as much as we say we do!"

Ashley's voice got louder. She pounded the podium with her fist. Her shoulder-length brown hair was pulled back into a low ponytail that swung from side to side with each thump, creating a more dramatic effect.

"There is strength in numbers! And thankfully, our systems of government are designed to submit to the consent of the governed, which is you! Not money, not power, not influence, nothing else! Mac Tabor only wants to make a quick buck, and he will do that at the expense of our community."

The crowd cheered. Dennis Kuntz was the loudest.

"Last night, I couldn't sleep. I watched my daughter, who was lying in her comfortable bed, and thought about our peaceful community. I moved to the country club neighborhood so I could give my daughter a better life. One where she could run around the street and be home when the sun went down, not worry about the traffic over three hundred new homes will add. I sat there and worried about my daughter getting hit by a car and how I was going to have to keep her inside."

Leah was doing a great job instilling fear in everyone. She spoke with a deliberate tone and made good eye contact.

"At five p.m. today, the city commissioners have agreed to meet at a larger location, the Agriculture Learning Center Building at City-County Park at the fairgrounds, in anticipation of a greater citizen turnout as they decide the immediate fate of the one hundred twenty-seven acres of golf course, restaurant, and pool." Her eyes lowered. "Mac Tabor and Chuck Shilling are supposed to be there. Chuck has agreed to put the contract signing on hold. So I'm encouraging you to grab a SAVE OUR COUNTRY CLUB sign." She picked up a sign that had been lying on the podium. "Take several, and give them to your friends and neighbors today. I, along with Mayor Burch and a few city council members, are going to be going door to door with these signs. Please. You have a voice. What Mac Tabor and Chuck Shilling did, going behind all of our backs and not getting the voice of our community, was wrong, and they should be held accountable!"

She smacked the podium, and the room went crazy.

It was my cue to get out of there. My first stop was going to be Mac Tabor's house.

THREE

I made my way over to Little Creek Road, which was located on the west side of town. There were only about ten houses on the right-hand side of the street, while on the other side ran Little Creek; hence the name.

I had to cross a small bridge over Little Creek. Eagerly waiting for me was the town duck, who knew I always had a treat for him. Today, he was getting one of the biscuits Mom had sent with me to give to Harriette.

I watched the duck devour the bread and give a little quack of thanks before he swam off down Little Creek, maneuvering his way around the rocks. I knew that at the end of the street, the duck would be waiting for me under the other bridge so he could get the other half of the biscuit.

I looked up from the bridge and down Little Creek. Neither the autumn sun and the crisp fall air nor the news of their neighbor Mac Tabor buying the country club would hinder the front porch ladies, which was what I lovingly called the four widow women who lived right next to each other. I could see that their blue-tinted hair was as shiny as the sun as they perched on Harriette's front porch.

My eyes feasted on the orange, yellow, and red mums planted in all of the yards. Neighborhood residents kept their yards nice and tidy, decorated with seasonal themes. Even Mac Tabor's house had a couple uncarved pumpkins sitting on the wall of his porch. And his house just so happened to be my first stop.

As usual, the ladies knew the time I generally came with the endless junk mail of the Publishers Clearing House, value coupons, and the monthly copies of *Guideposts* they eagerly awaited. They were going to have to wait a little longer today, because I had some questions about this country club deal for Mac Tabor, and I wanted answers. After all, Mac and I were practically family.

As the fatal night of Richard's accident played in my memory, I couldn't help but recall how Mac had been a good friend and insisted he go to the crash site and take care of what needed to be done there so I could focus on Grady. Mac had been great. He'd encouraged me not to look up the details online, because Richard's car had been so badly mangled that he knew Richard wouldn't want me or Grady to see it. That was why I'd never gone looking for photos of the scene or even gotten the report of the accident. The only thing that mattered was that from that day forward, ten years ago, I would be living life as a single mother to Grady and would never date or remarry. I didn't need to do that. Richard had been the love of my life, and I was his. It was unlikely to find that twice in one lifetime.

And here we were today. Mac was still single and always willing to help me out. He'd become a big figure in Grady's life. Mac had been there for every milestone: Grady's heartaches, graduations, and giving the father toast at Grady and Julia's wedding. So I couldn't help wondering why he'd kept a big deal like buying the country club a secret from me.

"Bernadette, you okay?" Mac answered the door without his shirt on after I knocked. I blinked a few times, a little taken aback at his physique. I had known it had to be somewhat good, since he did spend a lot of time with Grady at the football team's workouts.

He unlocked the screen door and pushed it open, his biceps bulging nicely.

"No." I gulped and busied myself with making his mail into a taco shape in my grip to hand it to him. "I…um…I heard…"

His gaze drifted down to my hand and the personalized letter on top of the pile. I recognized the handwriting from some previous letters. There'd never been a return address on them, only a postage stamp from the college town Mac had attended.

"You heard what, Bernadette?" He took the mail and stared at me.

"About the golf course. I mean, it's the talk of the town, and I can't believe you didn't tell me you're buying it," I blurted, sounding a little more hurt than I should have been. "You love that golf course. Are you really going to turn the land into condos? No one in town is happy about it. What about your company? If no one trusts you anymore, they won't hire you."

"Wait right here. Let me grab a shirt." He shut the screen door, taking a step back into the house. "You want a cup of coffee?" he asked. He thumbed through the mail, taking the letter on top with him.

"I don't want anything." I was careful not to have too much to drink while on my route. My bladder was the size of a peanut, and there were only a few places along the way where I felt comfortable using the bathroom.

Besides, one of the front porch ladies always had a glass of sweet tea waiting for me. I glanced next door to Harriette's house. The four widows jerked around as if I didn't feel their eyes searing the back of my head to see what Mac and I were talking about.

"Sorry about that." Mac walked back out. This time he wore a long-sleeved T-shirt and shorts, the perfect outfit for this type of seasonal weather. It was chilly in the morning and hot in the afternoon, only to return to cold at night. Mother Nature seemed a little more cynical in her decisions this time of the year, but it was still my favorite time.

"And you're not at work." I started right in on him as I leaned back on the porch's railing to ease the heavy mailbag off my shoulder.

"Whoa, let me sit down and get a sip of coffee in me before you go all postal," he joked, though I didn't find it very funny. "Okay, bad joke." He smiled and sat down in the Adirondack chair on his front porch.

"Harriette, what did he say?" I heard Ruby Dean trying to whisper across the yard, but it was hard for her.

"Turn up your ears so you can hear," Harriette spat back.

Out of the corner of my eye, I could see four little heads popping up over the brick wall on Harriette's porch. No doubt they were trying to get some insider information on the sale of the country club.

I returned my focus to Mac and watched as he took a few drinks of his coffee.

I always wondered why he was single. Mac Tabor was a catch, at least in the looks and friendship department. He had thick brown hair that he always kept nice and tidy, not too short but long enough to run your hands through. Not that I ever imagined doing so, but Richard would come home telling me all sorts of stories about how girls adored Mac and fawned all over him. Then there were his deep brown eyes that told you he had more than just looks. He had some brains and substance. His teeth showed how well-groomed he kept himself. They were as white as snow, and from the dental reminder cards he got in the mail, I knew he kept up on his appointments.

"Now, what was it that you're so upset about?" he asked.

"The country club and what it'll do to the people who use it." I dropped my mail carrier bag between my feet and sat down on the half brick wall that was built around his porch. I told him my concerns about the country club but left out how I was wondering why he was still single.

"First off, the country club isn't making money for Sugar Creek Gap. I've looked at all the numbers." He smiled.

Even with his hair all mussed, he still looked like a million bucks.

"No one in the fancy neighborhoods wants to pay the Home Owners Association fee to keep the pool and golf course running, so someone might as well buy it and make money. Dennis and Chuck have damn near gone bankrupt over it, and I'm the only one who can buy it. Why would I buy a dying country club and keep it when I can make money on prime real estate for condos?"

He let out a long, deep sigh and turned his gaze past me. I looked over my shoulder to see what he'd seen, because the disapproval on his face wasn't hard to notice.

The mayor, along with three of the city council members I'd seen just a few minutes earlier, was crossing the street with the signs I'd seen earlier under their arms.

"Stand with the citizens of Sugar Creek Gap against Tabor Architect Firm," I read out loud. "Wow. The whole town is against you. I just came from the emergency city council meeting. Did you know they've got a commissioners' meeting at the fairgrounds tonight at five?"

"They can't do anything. Just want to create a lot of ruckus for me. That's all." He was as cool as a cucumber as he dragged the coffee cup up to his lips, his eyes barely looking over the rim at the mayor and her gaggle of sidekicks. "Planning and zoning already approved it, though Dennis Kuntz is giving me a little problem. I don't know why, because he's going to make forty percent off my deal unless he has something else up his sleeve. I'm signing the paperwork tomorrow."

"Tomorrow?" I questioned, because I'd heard from Trudy that he was signing later today. But now I knew to chalk it up to gossip. This was why I had come straight to the source to get the real story behind all the tales swirling around out there.

"This deal has been a long time in the making. Dennis is always saying he wants to have something when he retires. If he takes my full offer at the signing, he can retire. He can get out of Sugar Creek Gap for all I care." He nodded toward the mayor and her crew.

"Well, okay." I pushed myself up and hoisted the bag back onto my shoulder. "I'll see you at the game."

"Yep." He got up from the chair. "I almost forgot." He blinked several times. "I can't believe it's been ten years. Are you okay?" he asked with sincerity.

"I'm fine." My voice cracked. "*Ahem.*" I cleared my throat and looked at my good friend. "You lost someone special too. Are you okay?"

"I'm all good, but I need to know that you and Grady are doing good today. I made a promise to myself when Richard died that I'd take care of you and Grady." He reached out and touched me.

I was thankful I had on long sleeves so he couldn't see the chill that ran up my arm. My mind was having a hard time processing what this was. There was no way I was attracted to Mac. I smiled, shaking off the notion that I could possibly have an attraction to Mac. He was honoring his friendship with Richard. I had been alone for so long, I'd bet if the duck touched me, I'd get goose bumps.

"We are fine." I took a step back, teetering on the top step. "I release you from your promise."

His large hand reached out and grabbed me by my arm.

"Are you sure you're okay?" he questioned.

"I'm just clumsy." I smiled and turned around so he wouldn't see me roll my eyes at how stupid I felt. "I'll see you tonight."

"Yes, you will." He pumped his fist in the air when I turned back. "Go, Grizzlies!"

Without another thought about the country club, I walked next door to Harriette Pearl's house, where the front porch ladies were all waiting for me.

"Morning, ladies." I greeted Harriette, Ruby, Gertrude, and Millie. They were all spread apart on different chairs with their hands busy with cups of coffee, chatting as if I hadn't heard them say *Here she comes, be quiet* when I unlatched the gate.

"We are good." Harriette smiled and nodded. "What do you have for me today?"

"Well, I've come with bad news." I frowned and reached around in my bag to grab her stack of what I'd consider junk mail.

"Oh no." Her gray brows furrowed as she appeared to be considering what it could be. "Is it about…" She hesitated and jerked her head toward Mac's house.

"Mac? No." I shook my head. "What about him? Did he have a woman over there?" I joked, knowing they were trying to get any news about his plans with the country club out of me.

"Who told her?" Gertrude jerked herself up straight.

A round of *not me* come from all of them.

"Wait." I was taken by surprise, getting stung by my own joke. "Did he really have a woman over there?"

"Mmmhhhmmmm," Harriette hummed through her pinched lips. "Young one, too. Not the first time she's been there, either."

"Really?" A bit of panic suddenly rioted through me, making me all confused. What was this feeling? Not feelings of being attracted to him. Maybe?

Nah. I continued to have a conversation with myself in my head as the four of them discussed this young girl with brown hair and a fancy car who had been crying when she left.

Maybe I was panicking a little, because if he did date or get married, where would that leave me and Grady?

"Bernadette, if his love life is not the bad news, what is the bad news you have for me?" Harriette stomped her black shoe on the concrete.

"I...um...I." I swallowed hard and blinked a couple of times. "You didn't win the Publishers Clearing House."

I handed her the mail and the box of biscuits, minus one.

It was no joke. Harriette filled out that sweepstakes form and ordered all the magazines. She was as serious as could be. I remembered when I'd see her at the grocery store when Grady was just a baby, and Harriette would pick up copies of different magazines, telling me how she swore Ed McMahon was going to be on her front porch one day with a big cardboard check made out to Harriette Pearl.

"That's all right." She eased out of the rocking chair. "I'll get the new one I filled out and your sweet tea." She held up the box before she went in. "We'll have these biscuits with Gertrude's jam."

I forced a laugh, still thinking about Mac's big lady news.

Ugh.

"I didn't forget you, Bernadette." Gertrude handed me a small glass jar with some fabric on the top tied with a little ribbon. "Jam for you."

"Thank you so much. You ladies are too good to me." I hugged her then took the empty thermos out of my bag and handed it to Harriette in place of the full one she was about to give me.

I hugged her before she sat back down in her rocking chair. "Now, for you ladies." I looked at Millie, Gertrude, and Ruby, referring to their mail. "Would you like your mail now? Or I can put it in your mailboxes," I asked.

All of them put their hands out.

I put my bag on the ground and sat on the top step to gather their mail. Plus, one stop for all four of them gave me a little time to chat and possibly find out more information about Mac's mystery woman.

"Mac didn't say a word about a woman." I shuffled through the mail, not because I had to, but it gave them time to give each other the side-eye and gather their thoughts.

"Millie thinks he's lost his mind." Gertrude nodded at Millie. The two of them were sharing the porch swing.

"I didn't say that, Gertrude. You are rude." Millie shifted on the swing, slightly turning away from Gertrude. "I just mentioned that it was out of his character to buy the country club to make condos when he loves Sugar Creek Gap so much. And now her."

"Something ain't right in his head." Ruby let out a long sigh as if it was normal to make such a comment before she took a sip of her coffee. "You, Bernadette Butler, are a fine woman. He needs to open his eyes to what is in front of him."

I shot her a look. My mouth dropped open then shut again.

"I heard Kenneth Simpson plum drove the golf course into the ground." Gertrude continued to gossip. "He spent all they had redoing the golf course and couldn't afford to pay the pool staff or the upkeep, not to mention the restaurant."

"Poor Audrey." Ruby tsked.

"Poor Audrey." Millie slowly nodded.

"Poor Audrey nothing. She'll be just fine. Your very own mama down at the Wallflower has been dying to get her full-time down there. She's the best cook in all Sugar Creek Gap."

Harriette always made me laugh. She told it like it was, and I appreciated that, but I was definitely going to ask Mama about Audrey and if she'd said anything.

"Looky here. They finally made it over to see us."

The mayor and her cronies were coming through Harriette's gate holding their signs.

"Good day," Mayor Leah Burch greeted all of us. Following closely behind her were council members Willy

Bingham, Ashley Williams, and Zeke Grey. "I'm guessing y'all heard about the country club issue. Well, we'd like to take a stand on it and bring this matter of making it into condominium living to a halt." Leah put one foot on the step and leaned on the bent knee. "I did see you at the meeting this morning. Shouldn't you've been working?" she asked.

It would be just like her to tell the postmaster how I'd slipped into the meeting when I was technically on the clock.

"I pertnear don't see that I have a horse in this race." Harriette pushed off the ground with her toe, rocking back and forth. "If they want to sell it and Mac wants to buy it, it's none of my business."

"But you don't understand," Ashley said as she moved around Leah. "My family and I live in that neighborhood, and if they make those condominiums, no telling what kind of riffraff will move in. We moved there for a nice community. Surely you of all people understand that, raising your family on this nice street."

"Then it seems to us"—Harriette gestured to her friends, who were all looking up at the ceiling as if they didn't like her throwing them under the bus—"and we all have discussed it," Harriette followed up in a louder tone, "maybe your little fancy country club subdivision should pony up and buy it yourself if you want regulations on who can and can't move in there. Or pay some sort of yearly or monthly homeowner fee to cover the cost of what Kenneth Simpson did to y'all. Seems to me that he had champagne taste on a beer budget."

"I never." Ashley huffed and jerked around.

"So you're telling me you don't want a sign in your yard?" Leah was relentless, making me wonder what on earth her beef was with the condos, but it wasn't my business. "Stand with the community."

"There's a commissioners' meeting tonight at five p.m. at the fairgrounds before the big game." Ashley was using any angle she could to capitalize on the situation.

"No way. Not in my yard. I happen to really like Mac Tabor, and I think he will make those condos amazing." Harriette gave Leah a look that made her blush and sent my heart racing.

"You don't stand with our community?" Zeke Grey spoke up, using Leah's same question. It seemed as if they were using it as a way of guilting the citizens who didn't care or didn't want any part of this entire mess. "That's not like you, Harriette," Zeke said.

He was Harriette's age, and they'd run around with a lot of the same people, so he probably knew her best out of the three council people.

"Zeke, my loyalty is to you and your family. When you ran for office, I sure did support you, and it didn't matter to me what your views were, but that was an election based on me being loyal to your family. But this here." She shook her finger at Willy Bingham, the youngest and newest member of the city council, who was holding the signs and not saying a word. "This is harassment to Mac Tabor, who has done a lot of good for the people of our community. It's now time to let the community rally around him, and that's what me and the girls are doing."

Millie, Gertrude, and Ruby all shifted uncomfortably.

"I don't hear them speaking up." Leah continued to poke Harriette. "They have voices. They can speak for themselves about their property, because the last time I checked the PVA site, you didn't own those three houses." Leah pointed down the street to Millie's, Gertrude's, and Ruby's houses.

"May I help out, Mayor?" Mac's voice floated across the yard. He was sitting on the brick wall of his porch with his coffee in his hand and a big smile on his face, enjoying the little fiasco taking place on Harriette's porch.

"Mac," Leah's voice softened.

"Come on, Leah." His smile faltered. "This is not a political gain. This is strictly a business move, and there's literally nothing you can do about it."

"Let's go." Leah turned to her three cronies after giving Mac a few long seconds of her cold stare.

"Just because you have money and can buy whatever land you want doesn't mean it's good for Sugar Creek Gap," Ashley Williams said through gritted teeth. "If I have to lay over the threshold of the lawyer's office tomorrow, you'll have to stomp on my body to get in there to sign those papers. And even if you do get them signed, we're going to find a loophole."

"Ashley, I'd sure hate to mess up that fancy suit you have on." Mac just couldn't let it go like I wished he would. "But it's pretty much a done deal." He held his coffee mug up in the air as if making a toast before he brought it to his lips and took a drink.

"You think you're something, but you're not!" Ashley's hands balled into fists at her sides. "I swear I will find a way that will stop you or put this whole thing on hold for a long, long, time. Mark my words." She shook a fist at him.

"Your threats today and from last night against me and Chuck Shilling were duly taken into consideration, and we decided to move forward." The more Mac addressed Ashley, the madder she got.

"Come on. We don't need to waste our breath on him when we can be talking to the people." Zeke Grey encouraged Ashley to join him, Leah, and Willy on the sidewalk outside Harriette's gate.

"I hate that man." Ashley stomped over to them, her voice clearly louder than normal. She definitely wanted us to hear. "Mark my words, one day he will get what is coming to him."

The sheriff's car drove up and parked at the curb between Harriette's and Mac's houses. We turned and watched as Sheriff Angela Hafley got out and stuck her big round brown hat on top of her head. Her eyes shifted between Mac's porch and Harriette's porch.

"Sheriff." Leah greeted Angela and took her foot off the step to stand tall. "We are leaving."

"Excuse me?" Angela seemed a bit confused.

"Someone call you?" Leah looked back at me and the front porch ladies.

"No." She shook her head. "I'm here to see Mac."

Mac walked to the steps of his porch and watched Angela come through his gate.

"What can I do for you?" he asked Angela. "Is this about last night?"

"What can you tell me about that?" Angela and Mac were doing some sort of back-and-forth conversation that left me in the dark.

"What's she saying?" Millie asked Gertrude.

"Shush." Gertrude glared at Millie.

"Why don't you tell me what you want to know, because there's nothing about last night that warranted the law being called." He crossed his arms across his chest.

Angela stood at the bottom of the steps. "It seems like someone spray-painted the golf course in orange spray paint." She took her hat off her head. "There's lines in the shape of buildings that have 'condos' written on them."

Mac's eyelids lowered, and his jaw slightly dropped.

"Where were you last night?" she asked him. "Where you at the golf course proving a point?"

"I had company last night. Chuck Shilling stopped by, and I had a female friend here." His eyes shifted to the side, and I could tell he was trying to look over my way.

"Mmhhhmmm," Harriette spoke up. "He did. But you did leave after the fight you had with both of them."

Mac jerked his head and gave Harriette a hard look.

"Where did you go?" Angela asked.

"I went to Madame's."

He went where? I tried like heck not to look at him. Madame's was a pub that had been a brothel when our little town was first founded. It was still a pretty seedy place, and I'd never even known he went there.

This entire morning was turning out to be something of an eye-opener. Ten years ago had been a relationship changer for me and Mac. His loss of friendship with Richard and my loss of a husband had brought the two of us closer. I'd considered him my best guy friend these past ten years. Clearly, he had a lot more secrets than I knew or he cared for me to know.

"You have eyewitnesses?" she asked. "If you don't, you better tell me, because I've got Judge Mason filling out some paperwork so I can get the security cameras of the homes around the club. The club isn't yours yet, and that would be vandalism."

"Chuck Shilling was there, along with my lady friend." Mac's chest heaved up and down. "I'll be more than happy to have them call you."

"See, this is exactly the kind of thing Mac does to our country club and town." Ashley held up the sign over her head. "Sheriff, you need to arrest this man right now!"

"That's one way to make good on her promise of stopping him from signing the paperwork tomorrow without her laying over the lawyer's threshold," Ruby joked, snickering under her breath.

Angela and Mac had already gone into his house.

"Now more than ever, we need to get the word out while Mac is detained. We can cover more ground if we each take a different street." Leah bobbed her head and smiled when the others seemed to agree with her.

Leah, Willy, and Zeke went back down Little Creek Road toward town, while Ashley finished off the rest of the houses on the cul-de-sac

"I don't want to watch her come back down here." Harriette kept one eye on Ashley as she passed Ruby's,

Gertrude's, and Millie's houses before she went to the rest of the neighbors on the dead-end street.

"That was something." Millie wrung her hands.

"It sure was." Gertrude was still watching the four of them walk back down the street.

"Mmmhhhh." Ruby rubbernecked around the porch columns to watch them too.

"This has been a big day already for Little Creek Road." Harriette was giddy with excitement. "I reckon I might go to that commissioner meeting tonight."

"As usual, I'd love to stay and chat, but I must be on my way." I turned to leave but felt a hand on my arm.

"Honey." Harriette handed me a little bag with tissue paper sticking out of it. "Did you think me and the girls forgot?"

My eyes stung with tears, and my heart felt a sudden emptiness that was hard to explain.

"We just want you to know we are thinking of you and little Grady." Millie stood up and hugged me tight.

"He ain't little no more."

Ruby groaned and took her turn to hug me.

"No, but we watched him grow up these past ten years into the man behind the Grizzlies!" Gertrude pumped her hands in the air before giving me a high five.

"Thank you." I pulled the tissue paper out of the bag and found a little guardian angel pin inside. "I will wear it every day."

I handed it to Harriette and let her place it on my shirt. I wasn't sure if she meant to put it right over my heart, but she did.

I felt all warm and loved inside even though it was a bitter day.

With a livelier pace, I quickly delivered the rest of Little Creek Road's mail.

All but one house—the last house on the cul-de-sac.

Mr. Macum. Boy…was he a pill. I'd never seen him with visitors, and he hated getting mail.

"Buster," I called out to Mr. Macum's dog, which normally greeted me at the gate. I always liked to announce my arrival when I knew an animal lived there, because I didn't want to get bitten if they weren't expecting me. Plus, it helped that I carried dog treats with me.

"Buster!" I hollered again. I heard him barking from inside the house, which gave me the go-ahead to walk into the yard and deliver Mr. Macum's mail.

I knocked on the door, because I had a special delivery to him from me: a stamp. He loved and collected stamps. Most of them weren't worth anything, but when I did come across a neat stamp, I'd ask the recipient if I could have it off their letter.

"What do you want?" He answered the door in his usual gruff manner. There were no mums or even a hint of autumn at his house, just dried-up annual flowers that had been planted for years.

"I have some new stamps I've never seen before and collected on my route the past week." I handed him his mail first then pulled out the baggie full of stamps I'd collected from the past week.

"Thanks." He grabbed the baggie and shut the door in my face.

"Can't make everyone happy with mail." I grunted and headed over the bridge that connected me back to Main Street from this end of Little Creek Road.

The sound of the duck quacking underneath the bridge brought me out of my thoughts about Mac. I couldn't help but smile knowing my duck friend was waiting patiently for me to throw him the last little piece of bread I'd saved for him.

I grabbed the other piece of bread from my mailbag and took out the thermos of sweet tea Harriette had prepared for me. I had a minute to enjoy watching my duck buddy eat his biscuit while I took a break to drink some tea before I headed back to Main Street and delivered the mail to the businesses on the mill side of the street.

I dropped my mailbag on the ground and took out the other half of the biscuit. I rolled my head one way and then the other to help ease the tension caused by the heavy bag before I rose onto my toes and leaned over the bridge to see my duck friend.

"Someone give you something to eat?" I questioned when I noticed he was pecking at something.

"Quack, quack," the duck vocalized and looked up at me.

My eyes glanced past the duck. He certainly was pecking on something someone had thrown over the bridge. But it wasn't food.

It was a body.

FOUR

"Let's go over this again." Sheriff Angela Hafley had me sitting on the sidewalk across the street, where the row of houses was located. "You came to feed the duck here; that's when you found the body."

I nodded, still a bit in shock.

"It's all right." Millie rubbed my back.

The front porch ladies had heard my screams, and I'd like to say they came running. They weren't able to run, exactly, but they did come humping it down the road as fast as they could to see what I was hollering about. Ruby had gone back up to Mac's house and grabbed Angela.

"Take a drink of the sweet tea." Harriette somehow had the thermos she'd given me earlier. The time from her house to now was completely a blur. "See, your guardian angel pin already saved you."

"Yep. You could've been lying dead down there." Ruby nodded with great big eyes.

"Ladies, I know Bernadette appreciates all your support, but right now, I've got to ask her some questions. Do you mind giving us a little space?" Angela asked them.

"I certainly do." Harriette's nose curled, and her eyes narrowed.

"Do you want me to stay?" Mac had also come down with Angela.

"I'm okay." I lifted my hand and took the thermos.

"If you're sure." Harriette had suddenly become a mother hen to me, which I truly appreciated. She looked at Mac with a threat in her eyes.

"I'm good. Thank you." I took a sip of my tea.

"She said she's fine." Mac shrugged and took the group of ladies a few feet away.

Barron Long, the county coroner, pulled the hearse tight up to the curb next to the bridge. I tried not to watch him as I answered any questions Angela asked me.

"Did you see anyone out of the ordinary on your route?" she asked.

"No. Leah Burch, Willy Bingham, Ashley Williams, and Zeke Grey putting out those signs is unusual, but you saw them." I recalled the mayor and the city council members. "But nothing other than that. I stopped to talk to Mac for a few minutes and then stopped at Harriette's, but as far as anyone driving or walking down here, nothing."

"What about any gossip that might make you think about a crime?"

"Crime?" I asked. Angela's question struck me as peculiar.

"The man we found in the creek—he's been shot." Angela plopped down on the curb next to me. "There's no weapon, and I'm worried this is a homicide. So if there's anything you can recall, I'd be so grateful if you'd tell me."

Baffled and dismayed, I took a few more drinks of the sweet tea.

"Do you know who it is?" I questioned.

"No. The body is facedown. We'll let the coroner look at it before we turn it over, so we don't have an ID just yet." Angela had always been a good sheriff, and she always played by the book. That was something I appreciated.

The wheels of the church cart squeaked, catching my attention. I looked up and across the street. Barron and another Sheriff officer were pushing the gurney up the embankment of the creek. The white sheet fell off the body.

Harriette Pearl let out a gasp that I was sure could be heard all across Sugar Creek Gap.

"It's Chuck Shilling," Harriette said in disbelief. "He left Mac's house last night, but not on his own recognizance. Mac pushed him out the door and down the front steps, leaving him lying in the front yard." Harriette shrugged. "Not that I was looking, but when you hear yelling, you tend to see where it's coming from."

"Harriette?" Mac questioned Harriette's outburst.

Angela and the other uniformed officer gave each other a look.

Before Richard died, I hadn't really paid attention to people's body language. After he died was when I started to not only pick up on others' body language but feel it. Literally feel it. All the sad faces, their words, their touches, their restraint not to touch…I felt it all deep in my bones.

Just like the chill Harriette's words had put in my bones. I shivered. There were so many things I had learned about Mac today. I wasn't sure I even knew him at all.

"Oh, honey." Harriette rushed back over and put her arms around me. "You're cold." She turned around. "Millie, go get Bernadette a blanket from your house. And hurry."

"Harriette," Angela called.

"Sorry." Harriette let go of me and took a few steps back. "I know, you need to talk to Bernadette."

"Wait, what did you say about Chuck and Mac Tabor?"

All of a sudden, the spotlight shifted off of me.

Harriette slid her glare to Mac. "He seems to have forgotten about that little part of his night."

Angela gave the other officer another look. I sucked in a deep breath as I watched him walk up to Mac Tabor. Mac shifted uncomfortably left and right.

"Yes. That's right. I heard them arguing last night. Now, mind you, I was not being nosy. That's not neighborly." Harriette was always nosy. Angela didn't need to do a Sheriff investigation to know that. "But when someone's fussing at ten p.m. and then doors are slamming, I wasn't sure if it were a robbery and I needed to dial 9-1-1, but when I saw Mac, no less with his shirt off, push Dennis down his front steps and then a young lady run out of his house crying....well." Harriette straightened up a little. "Let's just say it's something you don't forget right away."

"Come on. We are entering into a business deal." Mac shook his head. "We are in negotiations."

"You could see it was this man?" Angela asked Harriette, ignoring Mac's outbursts. "In the dark?"

"I might be old, but I can see. I've got twenty-twenty vision. You can go on down to Josh Adams and see for yourself." The pride in her voice made it clear she valued her vision at her age.

Josh Adams was our local optometrist. The doctor, eye doctor, dentist, and podiatrist, all in the same medical building on Main Street, were also my postal clients. They were generally the last stop on my route on Main Street, since it was the last building. Plus it was right next door to the post office, which made it nice to end my day there.

"I'll take your word for it." Angela had written some things down on her notepad. "And you know I'll also be asking Mac Tabor about it." With her chin still down to the ground, Angela looked up under her brows.

"Go on. Ask him." Harriette pointed to Mac. "He's right there."

I shifted around, snagging the butt of my polyester pants on the concrete curb, to see the officer putting cuffs on Mac's wrists.

I stood up.

"I didn't shoot anyone." Mac's jaw dropped, and his big brown eyes popped open. He looked back and forth between me and Angela. "Bernie."

"Sheriff." The officer who had helped Barron Long retrieve the body walked over, interrupting Angela by handing her the victim's ID. "It's confirmed. Chuck Shilling."

Mac jerked his gaze to the hearse. The back was still open. He hurried over there.

"This is ridiculous. Take these off of me." Mac lifted his cuffed wrists. "I didn't kill anyone."

"Mac, I'm not finished talking to you." Angela's voice boomed out, catching the attention of another officer by the vehicle.

The officer stepped in front of Mac, who put his arms down.

"Let me see the body." Mac shuffled back and forth to see around the officer.

"Barron, let him see the body," Angela hollered over to the coroner.

Barron slid the rails on the inside of the hearse out, the gurney coming with it. Gently, he lifted the sheet covering the man's face.

"Oh my God," Mac gasped and put his hand over his mouth. He turned his head to the side, chin down, and closed his eyes. From where I was standing, I could see his Adam's apple moving up and down as he swallowed hard to get control of his emotions.

Interesting. When Mac had come to my house after hearing the news of Richard's car wreck and death, he'd not acted this upset. Or maybe he was trying to be strong for me then? Wouldn't he try to be strong for me now?

Again, it was the body language that perplexed me. There were some buried secrets inside Mac. I'd thought I knew everything about the man. Obviously I didn't.

"Mac is private," Richard had told me once. "He has a life outside of Sugar Creek Gap, Bernie."

"I told you I had a feeling!" Iris's voice trailed down the street. Her long, curly brown hair with streaks of gray was piled up on top of her head in a messy topknot. "Mac! You're okay."

"So you're telling me you had an argument with Chuck last night?" Angela shifted her focus squarely to Mac.

"Yes." He looked over at me. Our gaze met. "But it was business. Not murdering business."

"Around ten p.m.?" she asked.

"Yes. I saw him at Madame's a little later, and he was just fine." He looked down at his feet. He rubbed his hands together. "Do I need a lawyer?"

She went in with the big question. "Did you shoot Chuck Shilling, Mac Tabor?"

There we stood—me, Iris, Ruby, Millie, Gertrude, and Harriette—all with bated breath. Millie hadn't even given me the blanket; she held it up to her mouth, her eyes big.

"Why wouldn't Mac be okay?" I heard Harriette ask Iris.

"I had a feeling." Iris's words caused a collective gasp from the older women.

"Mac, answer my questions." Angela's voice got sterner and a lot louder as she repeated the question.

"I'm sorry. If you want to question me any further, you're going to have to call Tim Crouse." Tim Crouse was a local attorney.

"Take him downtown." Angela twirled her finger in the air. "Mac Tabor, you're being taken down to the department for further questioning in the death of Chuck Shilling. You can call your lawyer when you get there."

"I'll call him," I blurted as the officer escorted Mac to one of the deputy's cars before putting him in the back. I wasn't sure why I wanted to take up for Mac when I'd been feeling as if he wasn't the person I'd grown to know and embrace over the past ten years. Before that, he had been Richard's friend, but now…I wasn't sure where we stood.

But for Richard's sake, I knew I had to help Mac out until I knew for sure he didn't do it.

The sheriff's deputy's car did a complete U-turn and zoomed off.

"I told you I had a feeling," Iris muttered under her breath as we watched the taillights disappear around the corner at the end of Little Creek Road.

FIVE

"Tim." I had called Tim Crouse.

The sheriff's department had the bridge at the dead end blocked off as part of the crime scene, forcing me to walk back down Little Creek Road to head back over to Main Street.

"It's Bernadette. Mac is in big trouble, and he needs you at the sheriff's department." I could feel myself starting to gasp for air as I tried to get out all the words.

"Sheriff station?" Tim questioned. "Oh geez," he groaned. "I told him that when the people of the country club found out he's going to put up condos, they were going to tan his hide."

"No. Worse." I gulped and ran across the bridge to Main Street. "Chuck Shilling is dead, and there's all sorts of people who overheard Chuck and Mac fighting."

"Dead? Chuck?" My news struck Tim speechless. "I...I...yeah, I'll walk over to the department right now."

Now that I could finish my route, I was in no mood for it. I stood on the corner of Short Street and Main Street, looking over at the old mill wheel. The water gushed over it with every turn. I looked to the left of it, where the courthouse stood tall. It was a large white courthouse, typical for the South, with a gold steeple on the top, the arrows of a weather vane pointing north, south, east, and west.

The Sheriff department was located in the back of the courthouse, and it was where they were questioning Mac about Chuck's murder. Angela would not let me in, but Mac had taken care of me and Grady when I was at my lowest point in my life. Now it was my turn to be there for him. Richard would think so.

The sound of someone knocking on glass caught my attention. It was Lucy Drake, the morning DJ of the WSCG radio station located on the corner where I was standing.

Once she knew she had my attention, she gestured me to hold on, flung her big earphones off her head, and met me on the sidewalk in front of the station.

"What on earth is going on over on Little Creek Road?" she asked. "I've gotten all sorts of call-ins about it. Plus I couldn't miss the deputy bringing someone to the department in the back seat."

Before I could say anything, Barron had brought the hearse to a stop at the stop sign.

"Oh my God. Someone died?" Lucy gasped, bringing her hand up to her mouth. She turned to me as Barron took a left on Main Street and turned right into the parking lot of the funeral home. "What happened?"

"Chuck Shilling was shot and killed." I gulped, still a little bit in shock. "I found him in the creek."

"Who did they haul in?" She looked between me and the Sheriff station.

"Mac Tabor." My voice trailed off. "I probably shouldn't have said anything."

"Wow. This whole country club thing has made everyone crazy." She shook her head.

"Why do you think it was because of the country club?" I asked.

"Because it's the only topic the callers on this morning's show wanted to talk about." She shuffled nervously. "I've got to get this on the news."

"Maybe you should wait. Mac wasn't arrested. He's just being taken in for questioning." All of a sudden, I felt as if I'd put my foot into my mouth. "Plus, he had no reason to kill Chuck. They were doing a big business deal."

"Nothing was signed yet. I got a call this morning during the morning chatter segment about how the deal wasn't supposed to be signed until tomorrow." Lucy had a daily segment in her morning show during which she let people call in to discuss anything and everything.

"That's true, but why would Mac kill him when they were both gaining something?" I asked what I felt was a reasonable question.

"Maybe the deal fell through at the last minute." Lucy shrugged. "I also got a call from someone who said they'd seen Mac at Madame's." Her right brow rose. "They heard Mac yell at Chuck before he left that he wasn't going to let him do that."

"Before who left?" I asked.

"Mac and some lady." Lucy frowned. "I'm sorry, Bernadette, but I'm afraid this isn't looking good for Mac."

"Well, he's innocent in my book until they have proof."

Just as I said that, Vick Morris , the radio station manager, ran out of the radio station.

"Who was the caller who said they'd seen Mac at Madame's?"

"Lucy, Chuck Shilling has been murdered by Mac Tabor," Vick interrupted.

"That's not true." I was starting to get a little frustrated with all the gossip.

"They found the murder weapon at his house." Vick shrugged and stepped out of Lucy's way as she ran back into the station, no doubt getting back on the air with this late-breaking news. "Now that Leah cancelled the special commissioners' meeting at the fairgrounds, I'm feeling pretty confident they believe Mac is the killer and the country club sale has stalled."

No meeting? I stood there debating whether to blurt out how I'd heard Ashley Williams say something to the effect of how she'd do anything to stop the sale or at least halt it until they could figure out what to do.

Anything?

Did that include murdering Chuck Shilling? And who had called in to the radio station?

SIX

Monica Reed was putting away the certified letters from yesterday's unable-to-deliver pile when I got back to the post office. Monica had long wanted a mail route job that would get her out of the building, but she'd never gotten one when she applied. It was good for me, because she jumped at the chance to take my route when I needed her to, which was rare.

"Monica." I grabbed one of the water bottles out of the big pack donated by the local general store. "It's your lucky day."

"Why's that, Bernadette?" Monica was doing exactly what I figured her to be doing, taking yesterday's packages and putting them in big plastic mail containers.

"I've got an emergency. I only finished the left side of downtown and the first five houses on Little Creek Road." I took my mailbag off my shoulder and took the mail I'd yet to deliver out of it. "Do you think you can finish my route today?"

"Absolutely!" She dropped the handful of packages she was going through into an empty container and grabbed the mail out of my hands.

With my route taken care of, I jumped in my old truck and drove straight down to the Sheriff station.

"Here's Bernadette Butler." Lucy Drake was standing outside of the back of the courthouse where the entrance to the Sheriff department was located. She had a microphone in her hand. "Bernadette, we are live on the air for WSGC. What can you tell us about how you found Chuck Shilling?" She stuck the microphone in my face.

"I…umm…" I stuttered and stammered before Tim Crouse pushed the Sheriff department door open and motioned me in.

"Well, folks, it appears Bernadette has Tim Crouse as a lawyer." I heard Lucy tell her audience what she perceived to be the truth…and that was how rumors were started in Sugar Creek Gap. "But let me tell you what she told me just about twenty minutes ago."

Though it did bother me because I was sure all of Sugar Creek Gap was now tuned in, I knew better than to let gossip get my goat. I'd dealt with a lot of it during Richard's death.

Still, I didn't like anyone to talk about me whether it was true or not.

"How is he?" I asked Tim once we were safely inside and away from Lucy's prying ears.

"He's being Mac." Tim didn't have to tell me any more for me to know Mac was shrugging it off. "He said he didn't do it. Maybe you can talk to him when they release him."

"They didn't charge him?" I asked.

"They are going to charge him, since they found the weapon, but I'm hoping to get him out on bail." Tim shook his head.

"How can I help?" I asked.

"I told Angela you'd give your official statement when you got here."

He walked me over to a desk, where an officer seemed to be waiting for me. There was a little silver case on top of his desk. I sat down in the chair and watched as he took out what appeared to be a fingerprinting kit.

I jerked around and looked at Tim.

"It's standard procedure to fingerprint the person who found a body so they can clear any of your prints from the crime scene." Tim still didn't make me feel better. "Or even the gun."

"I didn't touch anything." I shook my head.

"It's just a formality. Then all should be good." He gave the officer the go-ahead nod.

The officer reached for my right hand. He took each finger and rolled my pad on the ink, then pressed each one on the paper in the proper labeled grid. After he finished with the right hand, he did the left, then handed me a wet wipe to clean off the black ink.

While I cleaned my hands, I watched as the officer put the kit away. He pulled open his desk drawer, took out a tape recorder, and set it in the middle of the desk.

"Please state your name, address, and how you know Mac Tabor." The officer eased back in his chair and listened to me while I answered his questions.

"Tell me how you found the body." He wanted to know from beginning to end. I made sure I didn't leave out how the mayor and Ashley had made it very clear they weren't happy with the condos. "She should be a suspect," I half joked, but he didn't find it funny. Especially since she was ultimately his boss.

"Please just keep it to the facts," he informed me but didn't erase it from the recorder, which made me happy since it was on record.

Not that I thought the mayor did do it, but it got me doing some thinking…which sometimes got me in trouble.

SEVEN

"Think about it, Iris," I said to my best friend.

We were sitting at my kitchen table, rolling out the dough for the pumpkin sugar cookies I'd agreed to make for the Sugar Creek High School booster club to sell at the football game tonight. Iris had come by to help. "Maybe Ashley did do it."

I felt a low purr as my rescue cat, Rowena, rubbed up against my leg, curling her tail around the blue mail-carrier pants I'd yet to change out of. I picked her up and glanced over at the automatic feeder that dispensed kibble at six thirty a.m. and six thirty p.m. It wasn't six thirty, but she was hungry. She was always hungry.

"Why would she kill Chuck?" Iris did bring up a good question.

"Because he was selling the country club. " I took a few of the treats out of the cat treat jar and put a couple on the floor to tide Rowena over. I washed my hands and went back to making more cookie dough.

The treats must've satisfied my little tabby, because she jumped up onto the cat tree and stared out at the bird feeder I'd hung near the back patio to keep her company during the day.

I stirred the butter, oil, sugars, vanilla, eggs, and pumpkin together and thought about why she could be the killer. "She is leading the charge against it, not to mention I did hear her say that she was going to stop it somehow or stall it, even if she had to lay her own body over the threshold of the lawyer's office."

Iris used the round cookie cutter to make the perfect circle before she put it on the parchment paper on the cookie sheet. "Why are you trying to do the sheriff's job?"

"I don't know. I guess I owe it to Mac to prove his innocence." I put the ingredients under the mixer to make sure the dough was the perfect consistency that would bake up into a nice, chewy cookie. "I would do the same for you. You and Mac have been such good friends to me and Grady. I need to be here for him like he has been there for me."

"And how do you plan on doing that? Solving the crime?" She laughed and looked at me.

I looked back with a stone face. "Yes." The word fell out of my mouth without me even thinking about it.

"You're serious." The smile on Iris's face slowly faded away. She looked at the oven when the preheated timer beeped done. "And how do you plan on doing that?"

Iris stood up from the old farmhouse table and walked over to the oven with two cookie sheets filled with pumpkin sugar cookies. She put them in the oven and moved to the counter.

"I plan on talking to people." I wasn't sure what people, but people. I shut the mixer off and slid the lock knob to unlock, pushing up the top of the mixer to retrieve the bowl.

Iris and I both stuck our fingers in the dough to taste it to make sure it was perfect. We let it sit inside our mouths to let the ingredients mix with our saliva before we swallowed.

"I think it needs a little more pumpkin pie spice," Iris finally said.

"You're right," I agreed, reaching for the metal spice container.

"Good. You don't need to look into any murder." Iris was mistaken about what I agreed with.

"No, you're right about needing more spice." I shook the container over the mixing bowl. "Wrong about helping Mac. I'm going to start right now."

After a few final rounds of the mixer, I handed the dough to Iris to roll out while I grabbed my iPad.

"What are you doing?" Iris had dug her hand into the dough.

"I'm going to make some notes." I touched the screen to bring up the notes app as I sat down across from Iris. "You've seen it in those Hallmark shows. The person who solves the crimes is usually a baker or librarian, even a campground owner. Surely I can figure out something." The excitement of it welled up inside of me. "I'm a mail carrier. Don't you realize all the gossip I hear? I drown it out every day with a smile on my face. I get people's mail and know things they don't want me to know."

"And that's going to help solve Chuck Shilling's murder how?" Iris wasn't convinced in the slightest bit. She rolled the dough.

"It'll help figure out who heard what. It wasn't like Dennis Kuntz was quiet this morning." I recalled when I had passed the diner and he was outside with that toothpick in his mouth, his big belly full, talking about the city council meeting they'd had the night before. "I've got to go see Mama and see if Audrey heard anything and go back to the nursing home to talk to Vince Caldwell."

"I get Audrey, since she worked at the country club restaurant and has her side gig at the diner, but why Vince?" Iris walked over to the oven and flipped the light switch, illuminating the inside. She bent down to get a look at the cookies.

"He has never missed a council meeting. He Ubers to each meeting." I loved how Vince had embraced the new technology and not gotten complacent like I'd seen other elders do over the past ten years. "He will be able to give me some insight on what happened publicly between Mac and Dennis."

"Dennis?" Iris grabbed the oven mitts.

She took the cookies out of the oven and used a spatula to take them off to put them on the cooling rack. We had found that with the right amount of dough and the perfect temperature and baking time, the perfect cookie was made.

"Dennis Kuntz is Chuck...was Chuck's business partner. It wasn't an even split, and truly, he was just a financial backer to the failing club." I looked over the cookies, which smelled great. "He was just as determined to stop the sale of the country club as Ashley was."

"Let me guess." She watched me as I grabbed my iPad. "He's going in your notes too."

"Good guess." I leaned up against the sink and typed in my notes about Dennis.

"Those look and smell yummy." The hint of pumpkin, cinnamon, and sugar floated through my kitchen. My eyes took in the golden-brown edges of the cookie. I picked one up and broke it in half to look at the chewy middle. "Perfection."

I could imagine the faces of the customers who'd be buying some from the boosters as they bit down into the crunch, only to end with a chewy middle, sending them off into cookie heaven.

Iris made her special pumpkin spice glaze to pour over the top of them while I continued to type notes into my iPad.

"You've lost your mind." Iris shook her head.

"As long as we don't lose this game tonight." I quickly read through my notes.

Iris had donated some of her Pie in the Face boxes to transport the cookies to the concession stand at the high school stadium.

"I'll be sure to keep my ears open too." Iris looked up as she placed the cookies in the boxes.

"You're the best." I took a step over to her and hugged her. "You know as well as I know that Mac didn't kill anyone."

I headed down the hall of my little farmhouse to my bedroom so I could change into my jeans, Sugar Creek Gap sweatshirt, and tennis shoes.

"I know that you are passionate about it, and I'm going to help you." Iris's words put a big smile on my face. "Tell me what you know."

"Great!" I hollered out the bedroom door, quickly changing. Rowena had followed me into the room and was sitting on my dresser when I turned around to sit on the bed and put on my tennis shoes. "Too bad I can't have your keen sense to solve this crime," I told her and gave her a couple of scratches on the head.

My little ranch had been perfect for my little family of three. We had two bedrooms with a Jack-and-Jill bath between them. One room was mine and Richard's, the other Grady's. The hallway opened up into a large family room with a big stone fireplace and open kitchen.

I had a very comfy sectional couch with big slouchy pillows and quilts to snuggle up next to the fireplace on cold winter nights. There was a big-screen television mounted above the fireplace, where Grady and Richard had spent many Sundays watching NFL while I made chili and baked a sweet treat.

The farm table separated the kitchen from the family room. I had open shelves with very few dishes on them, since my family of three had dwindled to one.

I sat down at the farm table with my iPad in my hand. I scrolled to the top of my notes and started to read what I'd already written. "Let's go with the suspects one by one and their motives."

"Sounds good." Iris hit the timer button to stop it dinging when it went off. She took out the other cookies and scooped them off the sheet to put on the cooling rack.

"First we have Mac Tabor." I got goose bumps even thinking I had to keep him on the list for obvious reasons. "He had been seen having an argument with Chuck not only outside his house but also at Madame's."

"What?" Iris's mouth dropped open. She knew the bar visit was out of character as well as I did.

I shook my head.

"The murder weapon was found at his house." I used the pad of my finger to scroll down. "Ashley Williams is my next suspect. She's on the city council that's leading the charge for the citizens to stop the sale and the condos. She lives in the neighborhood, and she mentioned how she felt like their little community would be in for a lot of new traffic. She also said something about property values going down and how the dream of her daughter growing up in a great neighborhood is being shattered. She also got what she wanted with Chuck Shilling dead. No commissioners' meeting, and the sale is obviously on hold."

I remembered what Vick had told me in front of the radio station before I'd gone to give my statement to the sheriff's department and before talking to Mac.

"You mentioned something about laying at the door of the lawyer's office?" Iris inquired, making me happy that she was listening to me.

"Yes. Mac said Ashley had threatened him and Chuck." I nodded and typed it into the notes so I wouldn't forget. "Oh!" I snapped my fingers. "Ashley said that Mac had everything he got coming to him."

"What did she mean by that?" Iris put the last cookie in the box and closed it.

"I don't know, but if she knew Chuck was dead..." My thoughts started to put some theories together. "She killed Chuck and knew it looked like Mac did it, so he would be charged and the deal would fall through." I smacked my hands together. "And she spray-painted the golf course."

"Spray-painted the golf course?" Iris had yet to hear that little bit of news.

I quickly told her about how Angela had come to Mac's while I was delivering the mail and before I found the body and mentioned how someone had called into Lucy's radio morning show about seeing Mac and a woman at Madame's.

"A woman?" Iris's eyes popped open. "Who?"

"Yeah." Even after the few hours that'd gone by, my heart was still a little stung by that information.

As I told her about it, I grabbed the scarf Grady and Julia had gotten for me and used the guardian angel pin to secure it in place. We put all the boxes of cookies in my minivan. "Be good, Rowena!" I hollered back toward the bedroom, though I knew she didn't pay me any attention.

"Nice pin." Iris smiled.

"Thanks. The front porch ladies gave it to me in honor of Richard's ten-year anniversary." I ran my finger over it and truly believed I was being watched over.

EIGHT

The high school stadium lights could be seen all over Sugar Creek Gap. I dropped Iris off at the pep rally so I could get on over to the field to give the cookies to Eileen Dade, the booster president.

The campus consisted of all levels of education, with buildings for the preschool, elementary school, middle school, and high school. All the buildings were connected by an open-air walkway covered by a metal awning.

The sports complex, which spanned all four buildings, included a basketball gym, tennis courts, a baseball field, a softball field, and a football field that also was turned into a soccer and lacrosse field during those sports' seasons.

But it was football that made everyone crazy around Sugar Creek Gap, and tonight was our big rival game. Since I'd not heard from Grady, especially since it was our day-of-death anniversary, I knew he must be really stressed.

I pulled into the school complex and drove around to the back gate, where the ambulance waited for those just-in-case injuries. I quickly prayed there'd be none tonight or any night for that matter.

Eileen darted around the corner of the concession stand building and waved when she saw it was me.

"Let me help you." She came around the back of the van and put her arms out. She was the mom of a current football player, Samuel. Grady really liked the young man.

I took her up on her offer and loaded her up with a couple batches of cookies.

"These smell so good." She put her nose up to one of the cardboard boxes. "I might buy a whole box."

She smiled and turned around. Eileen's hair was long and black. She had the standard Southern girl look. If I didn't know Eileen was close to forty years old and had one child in high school and one in college, I'd have thought she was a college kid herself.

"Who are you kidding?" I took a couple of boxes myself and followed her inside the concession stand. "You might have a nibble, but I've seen you out here walking the track when Samuel is out there on the field for practice."

I remembered a few years back when Grady had said how he couldn't wait until Samuel got to be a junior and senior because he was on a whole different playing field athletically than the other boys.

"I have to keep up with these boys." Eileen took out a cookie and took just a pinch, just like I thought she would. "Tonight is a big night." She sighed.

"I know." I reached out and touched her. "I know I'm not supposed to know, but Grady told me."

"Samuel is so nervous." Eileen shook her head. "A big scout coming, and it would mean so much to his future if he would be recruited by a college and his entire school paid for."

"I know." I squeezed her arm. "He's smart and really talented. I'm sure once he gets on the field, his memory will take over, and he'll get out there to get the job done."

"I sure hope so." Her eyes grew big. She let out a deep sigh and clapped her hands. "Let's get the rest of those cookies."

"All right." I gave a hard nod and followed her back out to my minivan.

There were a few men on the boosters who had already fired up the grill. Soon the air would be filled with good-smelling beef burgers from the local cattlemen's association. The thought of them literally made my mouth water.

"Emmalynn Simpson won't be here tonight. She and Kenneth had some sort of argument."

When Eileen mentioned Kenneth Simpson, my ears perked up.

"Oh no. I hate to hear that." I was about to lay it on thick. "I thought they never fought."

"All this talk about Kenneth being the reason the country club went bankrupt has taken a toll on her."

"I heard the country club was going bankrupt, but I'd not heard anything about Kenneth." This could be a good motive for Kenneth Simpson to have killed Chuck Shilling. "Plus now that Chuck has been…" I hesitated as I remembered his body lying there.

My heart started to beat a little faster. There were so many questions rolling around in my head that wanted so desperately to slide off my tongue and out of my mouth that I literally had to pinch my lips together.

"Oh God, Bernadette." Eileen shook her head. "I'm so sorry. I completely forgot my husband told me it was you who found Chuck Shilling."

"It was awful." I piled a couple more boxes in her arms and grabbed a couple myself. I continued to talk as we walked back to the concession stand. "Needless to say, it was the last thing I thought was going to happen today. Especially since it's ten years ago today that Richard was killed."

"Geez, I can't believe you're here, much less still standing." Eileen gave me that look.

"I'm fine. Life still goes on." *Not for Chuck*, I wanted to say, but instead turned the questioning back to Kenneth and Emmalynn. "Why did Kenneth and Emmalynn have a fight? Is Kenneth a suspect or something?"

I figured if Emmalynn knew something about Chuck's murder or murderer, that would be good cause for them to have an argument.

"I have no idea." She looked out the door when we heard the band in the distance. This meant we only had a few minutes to get this concession stand open for business. "You think?"

"I just can't believe they wouldn't be here to see Teri cheer." I wanted to lay it on thick that my disbelief was of epic proportion. "I can't help but wonder if Kenneth is the killer, since he'd been accused for making the country club go bankrupt."

I decided to let that linger between us. I could tell by the blank look on her face that she was trying to process what I was saying. She took another cookie, which was completely out of character, and did something that was really eye-opening to me: she ate the whole thing without even realizing it.

"You know, Kenneth was spending so much money on redoing the course, he didn't even take into consideration what was needed for the pool or the restaurant. There are so many repairs that need to be done to the pool, I don't even think they will be able to reopen it." She shook a finger at me and leaned her hip on the counter of the concession stand. "Come to think of it, Emmalynn did say something about needing a lawyer for something."

"She did?" I put my hand up to my mouth as if I were in shock. "Oh no." I shook my head. "Poor Emmalynn."

Now that I'd planted a little seed in Eileen's head, I knew it was something I'd be able to come back and revisit in a couple of days. She was sure to ask Emmalynn. After all, Teri and Samuel were boyfriend and girlfriend.

"Here they come!" we heard someone yelling outside the concession stand.

We hurried back out to my car and grabbed as many of the cookie boxes as we could so we'd be ready for the crowd of fans walking behind the football team, who were walking behind the cheerleaders, who were chanting the high school fight song being played by the band.

The booster members lined up across from each other on the field next to the goal posts along with the early fans who had come to the game instead of the pep rally to grab a good seat.

Before I went to join them out on the field, I took my phone out and clicked on my notes, thankful the app synced to all my devices, and added Kenneth Simpson to the list. Now I had four suspects, all with good motives.

As I cheered my loudest, I could see that Grady's face was stern and serious. My gut fell to my knees as the pride swept across my face. I could've just cried looking at my strong, handsome boy. He had his game face on. When we made eye contact, I could still see the worry deep within his gaze. I gave him a Mom wink filled with love, causing a very slight upward curve on each side of his lips only a mother would notice.

He knew I had him in my heart no matter what the outcome of the game was going to be.

"We need to talk." Someone grabbed me by my arm when I wasn't looking.

"Mac." I gasped with relief when I saw it was him. "You're free."

"Yeah. Do you really think I killed Chuck?" His brows furrowed as his eyes searched my face. His jaw slightly dropped. "Are you serious, Bernie? I had to use my business as collateral to make bail."

"Of course I don't think you did it," I whispered. I walked away from the line of fans cheering on the team as they made it onto the field for the warmup. "That's why I have a list of suspects."

The band was playing the Grizzly fight song, and the crowd was doing its best impression of growling bears. It was so loud I could barely hear myself think, much less make my whisper audible to Mac.

Instead of trying to talk above the crowd, I motioned for him to follow me to my minivan, where I could use the excuse that I needed help with the rest of the cookies if anyone asked.

"Get in," I told him and walked around to my side.

"This is a nightmare," he started off as soon as we got into the van. "I have an alibi. I was..." He stopped and looked at me. "Suspects?"

"You have an alibi with a woman when Chuck Shilling was murdered?" I asked.

"How did you know?" He jerked his head around.

I wasn't sure why, but having him admit it made it feel like a betrayal to me even though there was nothing between us. He had been Richard's best friend, and there was no way after ten years that I was going to take it as anything but a charity-case friendship, though I did believe he loved Grady as much as Richard and I did.

"Harriette told me this morning how she'd seen you and Chuck arguing right before a lady left crying." I smiled when I noticed he was really bothered by me knowing. "Do you think you have to keep your love life from me?"

"Love life?" He rolled his eyes. "Some love life. I can't even find her to prove she was my alibi."

"One-night stand?" I knew she wasn't. Harriette had said she'd seen the lady coming there for quite some time. But if he didn't want to tell me, I wasn't going to beg him for the details.

"I've known her a while, but we had an argument that I'd rather not talk about." He looked down at his hands and picked at a hangnail. "I just want you to know that I didn't kill Chuck Shilling."

"Why did you and Chuck have a fight?" I wanted to know because I wanted to tell him that I was looking into who else could've had motive to kill Chuck.

"After the city council meeting last night, Chuck came over. Tasha was there." The muscles in his face tightened as he clenched his jaw.

So her name was Tasha. Ugh.

"He told me he wasn't sure if he was going to sell his part of the country club to me after all. He mentioned how he was getting some pushback from not only Dennis Kuntz but members of the community." He continued staring out the windshield.

The referees were walking onto the field with two football players from each team.

"Tasha and I…" He slid his eyes to me. There was a haunted look there that put a chill into my bones. "We…" He gulped.

I couldn't help but feel as if he was going to tell me something about his love life, but then he stopped.

"I…" He shook his head. "I just don't know."

"What don't you know?" I asked. I watched Samuel clap his hands and jump up in the air after they did the coin toss in the middle of the field.

My heart jumped. I knew Grady would be thrilled they had gotten the ball first. He had said that was how they would win: get the first touchdown and stay ahead. At least it had been his plan at the beginning of the week.

"I don't know what happened." Mac lifted his hand to his head and rubbed it. "I just know I didn't see Chuck after he left my house until the officer came and got me this morning."

"You had an alibi with Tasha?" I asked, though I wasn't sure I wanted to hear the answer.

He nodded a few times.

Mac didn't have any good reason for me to believe him without any concrete evidence to back him up, but for some reason, I did believe him.

He might've been telling me the truth about Chuck Shilling, but I had a feeling he wasn't telling me everything.

"I believe you." I reached over just as the other team kicked the ball. "And I'm going to keep my ears open during my route."

"I appreciate it." Mac turned to me and smiled. "You're a good friend, Bernie."

"You, Mac Tabor, are family." I gestured toward the field. "And if we miss any part of this game, Grady will kill both of us."

I noticed Mac didn't find my little joke as amusing as I did.

"Too soon?" I winked.

"Let's find the real killer first." He shook his head and rolled his eyes and put his hand on the door handle. "I guess you better get out there before the Grizzlies score the first touchdown."

"Me? What about you?" I asked.

"I'm not too popular around here right now. I'll watch from my car."

"Mac." I said his name to stop him.

"Yeah." He jerked his head around, his body half in and half out of the car.

"Why didn't you tell me about Tasha?" I asked. "Not that you had to."

The blood drained from his face. He took a hard swallow.

"It's not like Grady or I expect you to stay single and never have companionship. I'm just not sure why…" I could tell my words were making him uncomfortable. "…you would want to keep it from me. It's not like you didn't know I saw those letters. And they smelled pretty good."

"Listen. Mac stepped all the way out of the car and kept his head poked inside. "I don't even know what the relationship with Tasha is about, and in fact, last night, I had a real hard conversation with her, and I'm pretty sure she won't be coming around anymore. So we don't need to bring her up again. Tim is working on finding her."

"Oh." My eyes popped open.

"If there ever was anyone serious, you and Grady would be the first to know," he assured me and nodded his head toward the field. "Get on over there and root for our boy."

Our boy.

Why didn't it bother me when he said it as if Grady was ours?

NINE

"We won," I told Rowena when I walked into my house after the game. She was meowing and rubbing up against me. I picked her up and snuggled her close. "Samuel made three touchdowns. Your brother was very happy."

It drove Grady crazy when I called Rowena his sister. He liked her, but he hadn't grown up with her. We'd always had dogs on the farm, and after Richard's blue heeler had passed away a couple years after his death, I just couldn't bring myself to get another dog.

I spent long days delivering the mail, so it wasn't fair to get another dog who'd spend many hours at home alone. That would make me feel guilty.

I'd taken an extra route for one of the other carriers during their vacation a couple of years ago. The SPCA was on his route, and I fell in love with the little orange tabby that'd been turned in with a few little babies of her own. Rowena was only eight months old and had done all she could to nurse the three kittens. She was unable to nurse them due to being so malnourished, so the SPCA volunteers had to bottle-feed her babies, and I took in Rowena. I had told myself Rowena was just a foster cat and would go to a fur-ever home, not realizing she was my ticket to not being so lonely at night.

Rowena had wormed herself into my heart, and her stay ended up being permanent.

She jumped out of my arms, and I took the angel pin off the scarf before I took the scarf from around my neck. I dragged the scarf down the hallway, letting Rowena pounce on it a few times before she got her claw deep into the fabric. I let go so she could play with it and occupy herself while I did my nightly ritual. I washed my face and got my pajamas on before I grabbed the book I was reading and tried to get some sleep before my five thirty a.m. alarm went off.

"Mom! Mom!" Grady's voice echoed through the house.

"Hey, honey." I popped my head out the door of my bedroom and saw him and Julia standing at the end of the hallway. "I'll be right out."

"You scared me. You didn't stay after the game and after today…" His voice trailed off.

He'd remembered. I could tell in his tone that he remembered it was the anniversary.

"I'm sorry, Mom." Grady stood stoutly staring at me when I came out of the bedroom. He had a head full of curly brown hair. He looked exactly like Richard had at the same age. It was a blessing and a constant reminder when I looked at Grady.

Julia had one hand rubbing Grady's back, while the other was occupied with Rowena.

"I've been so wrapped up in the game that I forgot." His face was flushed.

"I forgot because of all the stuff going on with Mac and the office." Julia put Rowena down.

"I forgot too," I confessed in hopes of making them feel better. "Maybe it's time for us to move on from the date."

The three of us embraced, and I could feel the emotions building up in my baby boy. I pulled away.

"Enough of this." I wiped away the tear that fell down my cheek. "We have a life to live, and your father would've wanted us to celebrate your big win."

I moved past them into the kitchen.

"I've got some pumpkin sugar cookies for you two." I took the Pie in the Face cardboard box from the counter and opened it. "I saved y'all some." I put them on the farm table and sat down, patting the seat next to me. "Come sit down."

"What about Mac, Mom?" Grady grabbed the milk out of the refrigerator, and Julia grabbed three glasses off the shelf. "I can't believe I didn't hear that you found Chuck Shilling's body until after the game, when Vince Caldwell asked me how you were doing."

"We had no idea." Julia had gotten me some ice for my milk.

"Mac didn't do it." I broke the cookie in half before sticking part of it into my mouth. "I've got a list of people who could've."

"Why do you have the list?" Julia asked.

"Because I know he didn't do it, and I owe it to him to look around." My words made Grady look at me as if I had three heads and caused Julia to look at him with her big eyes wide open. "What?" I asked. "Mac has been very good to us over the past ten years. If I can keep my ear to the ground, find out a few details about why people wanted to kill Chuck—and there are many out there—then I'm going to help him."

"I don't think you need to do that, Mom." Grady gave me a tone and a look I certainly didn't like.

"I'm sorry if you don't think I need to do it. I'm doing it." There was no negotiation in my voice, but he kept on.

"You sound crazy." He pulled back and drummed his fingers on the table just exactly the way Richard used to do when I'd spent too much money.

"Don't you say that to me." I pushed myself up from the table. "I'm tired. Just because tomorrow is Saturday and you are off work, I still have to work, so I'm going to bed."

"That's it. You're not going to rethink this crazy idea of taking a murder into your own hands?" Grady stood up, and we squared off. He was about two feet taller than me, but I was still his mother.

"I'm going to keep my ear to the ground, that's all." It was apparent Grady was not happy with my decision, which just made me realize he didn't need to know everything I was doing.

"Grady, Bernadette wouldn't do anything to endanger herself. Besides, I'm sure she'll let Angela know if she hears anything." Julia tried to reason with him. "Isn't that right, Bernadette?"

"Of course I'd tell Angela. Anything to get Mac off the hook." It wasn't easy not giving into Grady, as I normally would, but I felt a strong conviction to help Mac.

"Mom, it's not looking good for Mac." Grady continued his campaign even as I walked them to the door. "He has a girlfriend."

"Tasha is not his girlfriend." I shrugged.

"Mom, he's been seeing her for a few months." Grady seemed to know more than I did. "People have seen them in town together. I asked him about her, and he told me that he'd introduce me when they took it to the next level."

I took a hard swallow and cleared my throat. "He told me they were over, and I really need to find her, because she's his alibi. So if you know how to get in touch with her…" I put my foot in front of the door so Rowena wouldn't run out when I opened it. "I'd love the information."

"She lives in Tennessee. That's all I know," Julia spoke up. "Do you remember when he was gone for that long weekend a couple of weeks back?"

"The fishing trip?" I asked. Richard and Mac used to go on big weekend-long fishing trips together. "With Tim Crouse."

"Well, he gave me his keys to the house so I could water his plants." Julia looked at Grady.

"Don't tell her this." Grady let out a long, deep, unhappy sigh and looked away.

"I'm telling her." Julia shook her head. "I wanted to let you know about it that weekend, but Grady insisted I keep my mouth shut."

"What happened?" I asked.

"While I was there, Tim Crouse called Mac and left a message on his answering machine. He said that he knew he was spending the weekend with Tasha, and he had the paperwork drawn up for her to sign. He said he was sorry he didn't have it in time for his trip to see her. Which reminds me that I still have his key." Julia's eyes stared into my soul.

"See, look at her." Grady threw his hands up in the air. "I knew you would be hurt, Mom."

"I'm not hurt." I tried to cover up the hurt I was feeling. "I'm just not sure why he'd not tell me. That's all."

Grady looked down at me with his big brown eyes with a little bit of hurt in them too. It was the same set of eyes that had looked at me when he'd run inside after skinning his knee or when his own feelings got hurt.

"No. I'm happy for Mac." I placed my hand on my chest. "He deserves to be happy. Which is why I need to find this Tasha person and help get Mac off the suspect list."

"Grady has some crazy notion that one day, you and Mac..." Julia stopped talking after Grady grabbed her hand.

"I'm tired. We've got to go." Grady bent down to kiss me on the cheek.

I stood on the covered front porch and watched the taillights of their car fade off down the driveway.

Julia didn't have to finish her sentence.

"Me too, Julia," I whispered the words.

TEN

I'd like to say I got a lot of sleep so I could be nice and prepared for the full day of walking ahead of me, but Mac, Chuck, and the entire country club situation weighed heavily on my mind, so much that I didn't even get one wink of shut-eye.

Even Rowena was sick of me moving around in the bed, leaving me at about two a.m. to find a more peaceful place to sleep.

I gave in to my restlessness and got ready for work. I didn't even bother making coffee because I knew it would be perfect timing to stop at the Roasted Bean on my way to work. I filled Rowena's bowl, grabbed a piece of bread for my duck, and headed out.

The Roasted Bean was a coffee shop on Main Street between the community center and Tabor Architects. It was perfect for me to park my car at the post office and walk across the street.

Matilda Garrison was the young and hip owner of the coffee shop. She had gorgeous long black hair she wore in dreadlocks. She'd grown up in Sugar Creek Gap but moved away to go to an actual roasting school located in the Blue Ridge Mountains of North Carolina. After she completed school, she worked there and saved up enough money to come back home and open her own shop.

"You're in here awfully early." Matilda was behind the counter, hand drying a few of the white ceramic coffee mugs. "I usually only see my regulars." She nodded toward a group of elderly people at a table in the corner.

The tables were at the front of the left side of the shop. There was a long counter on the right side with some barstools. The building had been an old-time soda fountain that had stood empty until Matilda revived it. The entire town had been happy to see she'd kept the original structure and interior.

"You're not delivering mail already, are you?" she asked as she put the mug on the hook with the others.

"No. I couldn't sleep with all the ruckus going on around here." I eased down onto one of the stools.

"I heard about Chuck." She shook her head. "It was a shame. He was just in here a couple of days ago with Ashley Williams."

"He was?" I asked.

"Yeah. I remember because he ordered a caramel frap, and she ordered one too. Normally she gets a pumpkin spice latte this time of year." Matilda smiled. "He even complimented that I had just the right amount of the good stuff, he called it."

"I'm glad you have that fond memory of him," I said. "Can I get a large hot coffee with cream to go?"

"Sure." Matilda turned and grabbed one of the white to-go cups.

"Did you hear what they were talking about?" I asked.

"I hear a lot of things." After she filled the cup, she opened the refrigerator and grabbed the creamer. "She was saying something about the country club. They were whispering."

She put the black lid on the cup and slid it toward me.

"On the house. I'm sure you could use the caffeine." She offered me a sweet smile and put her hands in the front pockets of her apron.

"If you recall anything you heard from Chuck and Ashley, please let me know. I'm really trying to help Mac out. I think someone is framing him." I picked up the coffee and took a drink before I stood up so I could head back across the street to the post office.

"Sure thing." She nodded.

Just before I walked out, Matilda hollered after me.

"Bernadette." Matilda hurried around the counter to meet me at the door just as I was about to walk out. "I did hear Mac and Chuck arguing a couple of days ago. Mac told Chuck it was a done deal and things were going through as planned, because he'd owed someone some money, and his investment in the condos was his way of paying them back."

"Mac owed someone money?" I asked to make sure I understood her correctly.

"Yeah. I thought he was loaded." She laughed. "Can't judge a book by its cover." She winked. "Look at me. See ya."

Gosh. Now I had more questions than I'd had before I went to bed. On one hand, I wanted to help Mac out so bad, but on the other, I was finding things out about him that made me wonder if I even knew him at all.

I pondered all the questions as I walked back to the post office with no answers to any of them.

Monica Reed was in the parking lot behind the post office.

"Good morning, Monica." It was still super early for any of the mail carriers to get there, but Monica was the main clerk, and she was always here by four thirty a.m. "What's going on?"

"I get to do a vehicle route today." She was inspecting the vehicle to make sure nothing was wrong with it. It was something all the carriers who used a vehicle had to do after they swiped their time card. They would be checking for flat tires, leaks, any damage, and so forth.

"That's great." I liked to see her get some time out from behind the counter. Sometimes dealing with the public could be brutal, especially if one had been at the window for five hours straight with no help and a line out the door. Grumbling mail customers weren't fun to deal with. That was why I loved my walking route.

"I already sorted your mail though," she told me on the way into the building.

That was part of her job as a clerk. She broke down all the mail and sorted it. It was my job to get the parcels, certified mail, and other special deliveries sorted according to my loop. I was lucky I was able to get my deliveries sorted by how I delivered my route. I always did all of downtown along with the small neighborhood with the front porch ladies as my first loop. Then I stopped back into the post office to get my second batch for the remaining stops on my route, the neighborhoods beyond the post office. I sort of wished I was doing the country club neighborhood so I could be a little nosy.

Then I noticed Mac had gotten another letter addressed in the same girly handwriting. I knew it had to be from Tasha and wondered if she'd written him a letter about the argument and why he'd said she was no longer going to be an issue in his life. I wanted so badly to hold it up to the light since there wasn't a return address and see if I could see anything, but that was illegal…if I got caught. Instead, I slipped it into my bag with the rest of today's first loop.

I was way too early for most of my stops. All but one—the Sugar Creek Gap Nursing home.

It was the only place where customers weren't waiting on me. Half the time, their mailboxes were still full from the previous day's delivery or beyond.

"You're here awfully early." Vince's voice cause me to jump around.

"Vince." I gasped and put my hand up to my chest when I noticed him in the wingback chair near the entrance of the building. "I didn't see you there."

"I usually start my day here and then take my coffee out on the porch." He dog-eared the newspaper he was reading and looked over it. "I read here that you are the one who found Chuck Shilling."

"It was awful." I walked over to him and took a seat in a matching chair next to his. "I never thought my day would end up like it did after I left you that morning."

"I saw you at the emergency meeting." He rested his arms in his lap. The paper crunched shut. "You think your friend Mac Tabor did it?"

"Heck no." I shook my head. There were a lot of things I was realizing I didn't know about Mac Tabor, but I knew he wasn't a killer. "And I've vowed to keep my eyes and ears open to figure out who just might've killed Chuck, because a lot of people had reason."

"Is that so?" Vince's tone made me think he wanted to hear more.

"For instance, I overheard Chuck's business partner saying how he was not happy with Chuck and they'd gotten into an argument the night before. He could've been keeping an eye on Chuck, and when he saw Chuck leave Mac's, he confronted him and killed him. I'm not sure what their contract would've said about Chuck's sixty percent of the country club, but I'd assume it'd go to Dennis. That's motive."

Vince shrugged as if he wasn't convinced.

"What?" I asked.

"It all depends on if Dennis has an alibi. How did Chuck get to the bridge? Was he killed there? Dumped? How long had he been there? Shot at close range? Far away?" Vince asked all sorts of questions.

"You, my dear friend, have been watching too much of that one channel." I snapped my fingers to try to remember.

"MeTv?" He laughed. "That's a great channel, and I love *Matlock*, but nope." He rubbed his knees with his hands. "I'm a retired agent with the FBI."

"Good one." I laughed and dug through my mail to get his out.

"I'm serious." He didn't smile like he normally did. "I've been retired for fifteen years now. I'm not from here, as you know, and when I left the Bureau, I wanted a small, quiet little town with a good view."

"You're not joking." I sat back up and looked at him. "You're serious."

"As y'all say around here, as a heart attack." He smiled. "That's why I don't think Dennis Kuntz did it. He wouldn't be going around making all sorts of veiled threats. And…" He hesitated. "I've done a little digging of my own."

"You have?" This really got my interest piqued.

"Dennis Kuntz's mother lives in the assisted part of the facility." He nodded toward the door. "I sit on that porch every single night to watch the sun set. Every single Thursday night, Dennis Kuntz comes to visit his mother. They watch *Jeopardy*, and he usually watches a few other shows with her until she falls asleep."

"Then he'd been awake to have killed Chuck. Maybe he was driving down Main Street and saw Chuck. They took a walk." I was throwing things out there. "We do know…" I grabbed my phone from my back pocket and pulled up the notes. "Thursday night, Mac Tabor had Tasha over to his house after the city council meeting. Chuck Shilling stopped by Mac's house to tell him he wasn't sure if he was going to go through with the deal because the town had gone nuts. Then Tasha and Mac had a fight, she left, and Mac followed her to Madame's."

"Madame's? Whoa." Vince's eyes lit up. "I've always wanted to get an Uber there."

I rolled my eyes and sighed.

"Anyways, Mac claims Chuck was there. That's the last time he saw him alive." I put my phone down and looked at Vince.

"What else do you have on that phone?" He leaned a little closer.

"Well, I have Ashley Williams as a suspect because she lives in the neighborhood. She claims that she'd do anything to stop the sale of the club because of the riffraff and traffic it would cause, but I think her main motive is her family." The more I talked out loud, the more my theories started to come together cohesively. "She said they moved there to bring their daughter up in a great community. She wants that life, and like my mama said, when people's lives get turned upside down, they don't know how they are going to live in them, and that's motive enough."

I scrolled down a little more.

"I hate to even think maybe Kenneth Simpson had something to do with it." There was a twinge of sadness when I thought about him and Emmalynn. They were such nice people, but nice people sometimes did bad things. "He's the golf pro there and apparently being blamed for the bankruptcy of the country club. I'm going to ask

Audrey about them today when I drop off some of the leftover pumpkin sugar cookies. And it just so happens Emmalynn said they had a meeting with a lawyer about some important business." I could see by the look on Vince's face that he was taking it all in. "They even missed their daughter cheering last night to take care of this business. That's suspicious to me. Plus his reputation has been dragged through the wringer, and if the club did go under, who is going to give him a good recommendation?"

"You've done your due diligence." Vince sat back and drummed his fingers over his belly.

"Which makes me wonder if he or Ashley were the ones who spray-painted the golf course." I wiggled my brows and typed that into my notes so I wouldn't forget.

"The only way to see if any of your theories are true is to snake them out." Vince's eyes twinkled.

"You're enjoying this." I smiled and gave him the side-eye.

"It's not easy living a life of detective work and then retiring. That's why I go to all the council meetings and trials down at the courthouse. Keeps me in the game without being in the game." A slow smile crossed his lips.

"Not that I'm happy anyone was murdered, but I can't help but think I'd like to get in on a little sleuthing myself."

"Like partners?" I asked.

"Yeah. You are the eyes and ears on the street. I've got connections." He leaned over a little like he didn't want anyone hear. Like there was even someone up this early to hear us. "I even have my online logins from being with the bureau." He snickered. "I guess I was an oversight." He winked.

"Like secret things?" I asked, having no idea what I was even talking about. His actions made me think it was very important though.

"I've got ways of finding things out about people and money, things that might help us figure out why so many people are against the club. Things that might help us hack into security cameras, like the ones at the country club."

His words made my jaw drop. "You mean you can break into the country club cameras to see if a certain someone was spray-painting something?" I asked.

"I'm not saying I'll be able to jump on the library computer here at the nursing home and get it immediately, because I might be a little rusty, but I'll be able to figure it out." He winked, folded the paper up, and set it on the small round table between us. "Deal?" He stuck out his bony little hand.

"Deal." I gave him a good handshake. Or thought I did.

"You aren't going to break my bones." He kept his hand extended. "We are partners, and I need a firm handshake."

"You are something else, Vince." I did exactly what he asked to seal our deal. "So, now what?"

"First, you need to find out everything about Mac's night and find the woman. We not only need her account of Mac's whereabouts to help me out, but she might've seen something at the Madame he didn't."

Vince was asking me to do something that was pretty tricky, considering the situation of my friendship with him.

"Okay." I nodded in agreement even though I had no idea how I was going to approach this situation. "I can do that."

"Then you need to see Gill Tillett down at the General Store. We need to know who bought spray paint." His eyes lowered as if a thought had come into his head. "I'm thinking this is a local job, the murdering, and probably a little premeditated if someone went to all the trouble to get a gun from Mac's house. You need to ask all them widow women if they heard anything else that night."

"Okay." I nodded and realized there was going to be a whole lot more to this sleuthing than I even thought.

"I'm going to need you to also get me one of those burner phones from the General Store." He reached around and pulled a hundred-dollar bill from his wallet. "We are going to have to communicate somehow, and I don't want it traced back to me."

"Got it." I took the money.

"You just come back here after your work shift and give it to me along with reporting in on what you found out." His eyes twinkled. I could see the excitement and thrill this type of work gave him.

After the plan we made, I was able to get the mail delivered to all the little mailboxes. I also took the time to write down in my notes app exactly what Vince wanted me to do so I didn't forget something.

I did wonder why he'd not addressed me finding out anything about the other suspects like Dennis Kuntz, Ashley Williams, or Kenneth Simpson. He was the expert, and maybe it was some sort of way the FBI weeded out the little things, so I went along with him, and happy to do it.

I ran my hand over the outside of my mail carrier bag, knowing the new letter for Mac was in there. I certainly was looking forward to finding out exactly who Tasha was to Mac.

ELEVEN

The courthouse opened at seven a.m. on Saturday and closed at noon. This was the only day I reversed my downtown loop and started with the courthouse first. Normally, I delivered the mail to the nursing home last, but this was not a normal day by any stretch of the means.

I tugged the edges of my scarf up around my neck and put my hands in the pockets of my jacket. The weather was changing fast, and a bitter wind was coming in, which told me the first signs of winter were coming.

The old mill echoed its groans with each turn, giving Main Street an eerie feel. The lampposts glowed in the dark. The sunrise wouldn't show itself for another half hour. I loved the fall, and when I did this route on Saturdays, I generally enjoyed the quiet peace and serenity of the water rushing over the wooden wheel.

But today, there was something in the air that brought goose bumps along my spine, and they weren't caused by the chilly wind.

It was as if I felt someone watching me.

I hurried down the sidewalk as quickly as I could and passed all the shops I'd be visiting around the nine a.m. hour when they opened. The lights from inside the courthouse glowed, a welcome sight once I was past the old mill.

Once inside, I stopped briefly at the door and let out a long sigh, happy the courthouse opened early every morning.

"That was a loud sigh." I heard Trudy Evans before I'd even seen her.

"Hey, Trudy." There was a bit of relief when I saw her.

"You okay?" She looked at me with a cup of coffee in her hands. "Here. You look like you need this more than me."

"That's okay. You know, with finding a body and all, I might be a little creeped out." It sounded so dumb to be scared.

"Honey, there's a killer on the loose if you don't believe Mac did it." She walked over and handed me the coffee. "And I'm not so sure the sheriff's department thinks he did do it."

"Why do you say that?" I questioned, keeping my ears open like Vince had told me.

"Because that coffee." She pointed to it. "I get it every morning from the sheriff's department, and this morning I overheard someone saying the preliminary autopsy was back, and Chuck was killed at close range. No fingerprints on the gun. One of the officers said it looked like someone wiped the prints off, which doesn't make sense if it's Mac's, because his prints would be all over it since it's in his house and he put it there." She took a step closer when someone came through the doors of the courthouse. "They didn't find the gun in Mac's house. It was in the bushes next to his front porch."

"You're kidding." My jaw dropped. There was so much information in what Trudy had told me that I wasn't sure if I needed to go back and tell Vince or just keep going about my day and check off the list of things he wanted me to do.

"What else did you hear?" I asked her.

"Nothing," she snarled. "They caught me listening in. One of them said, 'Ain't you got to get to work, Trudy Evans?'" She rolled her eyes then waved her hand in the air. "Which I do. You enjoy that coffee and stay safe out there." She winked and smiled. "There is a killer on the loose."

I didn't find anything funny in any part of her saying there was a killer on the loose. It didn't entertain me in the least bit, but this little bit of gossip she gave me could help in Mac's case.

After I delivered the mail to the various branches of government in the courthouse, I walked up the big marble steps to where the businesses who rented from the local government were located. I was looking for Tim Crouse specifically.

"Any mail today?" I asked Tim when I popped into his office.

"Not today, Bernadette." He took his glasses off and set them on top of his desk. "Have you talked to Mac?"

He gestured for me to sit down. I did and put the mailbag on the floor between my legs.

"I talked to him at the game last night." I took a sip of the coffee. "How's the case?"

"I can't really discuss it with you, but he's going to need a friend to lean on." The corners of Tim's eyes dipped. He looked as if he knew something that he couldn't tell me, and it made me worry Mac was guilty.

"What about Tasha?" Not only didn't I expect him to really answer me, but I didn't expect the shocked reaction on his face. "Have you found her? Mac was with her the night of Chuck's murder, and I'm assuming you'd want to question her."

"Mac told you about Tasha?"

"Listen, Mac has been amazing to me and Grady. Grady is off and married. A grown-up. And just in case you hadn't noticed all the bags under my eyes, lines around them, and this"—I pointed to my chin— "I'm an old broad. I didn't expect and never wanted Mac to stay single and feel like he needed to take care of me and Grady."

"It's the friendship." A little snort of laughter escaped Tim's nose. "I wish I had as good a friend as Mac was to Richard…and you."

"So did you get in touch with her?" I wondered but left out the part about the papers he wanted Mac to have her sign.

"Her phone has been turned off." He drummed his fingers on the top of his desk. "I'm guessing she wants nothing to do with Mac or this investigation."

He only fueled me more to find out what really happened to Chuck Shilling.

"What if she doesn't want anything to do with it because she knows something? Good or bad?" I shrugged.

"Whose side are you on?" I knew he was joking, but my loyalty should never be questioned.

"Mac's, of course. Or I wouldn't be going through a list of suspects I've collected." I probably shouldn't've told him that.

"What list?"

Yep, judging by the look on his face, I should've kept my mouth shut.

"I've been doing a lot of thinking. I hear things as a mail carrier. I can't help but think that Ashley Williams could've done it because she's leading the charge to stop the condos going up. She framed Mac. Plus, she's been very vocal about how nothing is going to stop her even if she has to lay over your threshold." I pointed to his door. "Then there's Dennis Kuntz. He's got everything to gain because I'm sure he's going to get all of Chuck's part now that Chuck is dead."

Tim leaned back in his chair and drummed his fingers together.

"What about Kenneth Simpson? He is being blamed for the country club going bankrupt, forcing them to sell it. Plus, Emmalynn and Kenneth didn't show up to watch Teri cheer last night, which is odd. They've come to every game." The words continued to spill out of my mouth as if my brain was doing some sort of dump. "Emmalynn told someone they weren't coming because they needed to see a lawyer. Now, were they seeing a lawyer because they knew it was only a matter of time before Kenneth was named Chuck's killer?"

"No, they needed a lawyer to be sure they could get out of his contract at the country club so he could take a job in North Carolina, which is where they've been the past two nights." Tim leaned up and rested his elbows on his desk. "I'm that lawyer."

"Oh." Dang. I mentally crossed him off my list.

"And Dennis Kuntz doesn't gain anything from the contract. Chuck's son will take over his part of his father's businesses, including all contracts." Before I could say maybe it was the son who had some sort of financial gain, Tim stopped me. "His son has a solid alibi. Angela has already gotten this information from me."

"It still doesn't mean Dennis Kuntz didn't kill him." I shrugged.

"True. But you really need to leave it up to Angela and the sheriff's department." It was written all over Tim's face that he didn't like me snooping at all.

I changed the subject when I knew he wasn't going to budge on Mac and Tasha's relationship. "I guess it's good news about no prints on the gun."

He perked up. "How do you know that?"

"Umm…" I took another drink of the coffee. "I just heard it downstairs."

I wasn't going to reveal my source because I didn't want Trudy or the officers who were talking to get in trouble.

"Just now?" He looked over at the clock on his wall.

"Right before I came up here."

I noticed him look at the coffee cup I was drinking from.

"That cup is from the sheriff's department." He snapped his fingers. "Listen, I've got to make some calls. Be sure to stop by and see Mac."

"Oh, I plan on it."

I stood up, happy that he didn't press me any further. I lugged the mailbag over my shoulder and threw the coffee away in the trash receptacle in the hallway before I delivered the rest of the mail to the businesses on the floor.

The next stop was the sheriff's department. When I walked in, no one was there. I really wanted to see if I could get as lucky as Trudy had and overhear something, but that wasn't going to be possible. They had a few pieces of mail in their outgoing basket, so I grabbed them, tossed them into my bag, and headed out. I was happy to see the sun popping up over the mountains, making the outside not so scary anymore.

TWELVE

The only stores with lights on were the Wallflower Diner and Tabor Architects. Both employed people I wanted to see. Since Tabor Architects was the first one I came to, I headed inside.

"Good morning," Julia greeted me. "You're early today. Did you stop by the diner and see Grady?"

"No. My next stop." I reached around the mailbag and grabbed their mail, which was just a monthly architectural magazine Mac subscribed to. "How's Mac?" I asked when I noticed a light coming from underneath his office door.

"He's not doing so good. I think he stayed here last night." She didn't sound sure. "He's on the phone with some clients who haven't paid. He said he's going to need the money for his defense."

"Did they charge him with the murder?" I asked, wondering if it was a new development.

"Not that I know of, but he told me to finish the billing for this past week and just go home for the day." She picked up the stack of papers. "I've already done these and only have a few more left."

"Then you and Grady can go have some fun." I loved when the two of them could spend some time together.

"We planned on doing a little hayride and romantic supper before the cold weather really hits."

It was so nice to see how much she loved Grady. It was exactly what a mother wishes for her son, and Julia was a blessing to our family.

"That sounds like a lot of fun. But don't forget tomorrow night's Sunday supper," I reminded her.

Every Sunday, I have my parents, Grady, and Julia over for supper. It was a long-standing tradition I'd been continuing since I took over my parents' farm. Richard had loved the parents. Some Sundays he missed because he'd have to leave town for work so he'd make it to his early-morning Monday meetings. But he wanted every single detail when he'd call on Sunday night before he went to bed.

"I'll be right back." Julia popped up from her chair and went to the bathroom.

I couldn't help but notice the keys sitting on her desk. I knew they weren't hers because I didn't see the monogrammed keychain I'd given her, but this set might be the one she said Mac had given her for housesitting.

For a split second, I debated whether it was ethical if I took them and sorta let myself into Mac's house while he was here. Apparently, I wasn't too ethical, because I wanted to find those letters from Tasha. I'd like to say I wanted to find them so I could find her like Vince wanted me to, but if I was being honest with myself, it was strictly because I wanted to know what was in them and if they were having a relationship.

I grabbed the keys and slipped them into my bag.

"I wanted to make sure Mac was occupied before I gave this to you." Julia handed me an envelope. "Not that I want Grady to get mad at me for snooping, but I did a little digging around this morning and found Mac's business plan for the condos. It appears as if he's going to sell them as soon as he builds them. This could be a reason someone is trying to set him up."

Judging from the sound of Julia's voice, she was on board with my sleuthing around, unlike my son.

She looked over her shoulder. When she saw it was clear, she looked back at me. "I think he's in financial trouble. He's trying to pay off something, but it's cryptic in the system." She frowned. "I'm sorry I'm not more helpful today."

"Maybe this was why Chuck Shilling didn't want to go through with the deal. He knew Mac was just going to turn it and make a profit, which wouldn't be good for our community." I tried to shrug off the gut punch, but I felt sick to my stomach. This was a whole different situation than just a murder.

Julia excused herself again.

That was when I headed out the door. It was still early enough that the front porch ladies might not be out, and that was probably best if I was going to sneak into Mac's house.

There was one problem. Rushing over to Mac's house while he was at the office would put me off schedule for my delivery route, and when I was off schedule, it made for cranky customers. Literally, I had customers who sat next to their window or even greeted me on the street. I was willing to have cranky customers so I headed right on over there.

I knew my little duck friend would hear me when I crossed the bridge to head on over to Little Creek Road, so I grabbed the extra slice of bread I'd taken from home and tossed it into the creek after I heard him give a few quacks.

"I can't hang out this morning," I told the duck. "I've got a murder to solve. And don't swim down to the other bridge, because I won't be there for a while."

I laughed and wondered if Iris was right about me needing some sort of companionship. The extent of my day consisted of talking to a duck.

The entire street was still asleep. The small frosted globes on the front porches next to the doors were glowing in a line when I looked down the row of houses. I was glad to see Mac didn't have his front porch light on, because the darkness would make it much easier to slip in without being seen.

It was the creaky gate that generally got the neighborhood dogs barking or the ears of the front porch ladies to perk up. I slowly opened the gate and tried to push up or down on it to lessen the noise. I made sure I didn't make any sudden moves in case someone was watching out their windows and saw my shadow. I wore big thick-soled shoes for walking, so I knew those would be nice and quiet as I tiptoed up to the front porch. It was then that I darted up the stairs, confident I hadn't been seen.

The key was ready in my hand, and I jammed it into the lock. Inside, it was completely dark, so I dragged my phone out of my pocket and hit the flashlight feature. I set my mailbag on the floor next to the front door so I didn't have to lug the thing.

The wooden blinds on all the windows were shut, so I wasn't worried about someone seeing my flashlight.

"What are we looking for?"

The shaky voice startled me.

"Oh my gosh! Harriette!" I saw her standing in the open front door when I turned the phone flashlight on her. "You scared me."

"You scared me sneaking through Mac's gate like that." She put a hand on her waist. Her housecoat swung from side to side. "So, what are we looking for?"

"Letters." I walked over and hurried her past the threshold so I could shut the door. I did take a quick look outside to see if any of her other friends would be joining us. "Letters from Tasha."

"That woman he's been dating?" she asked. I nodded. "Why?"

"She might have some information that'll help Mac. She was with him the night of Chuck's murder, and she's his alibi. Only he can't get in touch with her. Tim Crouse said her phone has been disconnected. I also heard Chuck,

Mac, and Tasha were all at Madame's after they had the fight you saw."

"Then I reckon we better get to looking." She pointed to Mac's home office that just so happened to be located on Harriette's neighboring side. "He works in here a lot, and I've seen him open his mail in here a time or two."

I shot her a questioning look.

"What?" She shrugged and pushed past me. "I like to know my neighbors are safe, and if I'm outside on my porch or sitting at my kitchen table, I can't help it if I can see over here. Do you want me to wear blinders?"

"Did I say anything?" I asked and followed her into the office. "If you can help me find Tasha, then it's all good."

Harriette was already opening and shutting the drawers of the desk. There were a lot of rolled-up building plans in the corner of the room next to what he called his planning desk, which had a cantilevered top with an overhead lamp clamped to the edge of it.

"This looks like her." Harriette picked up a photo showing Mac laughing next to a younger woman. "They look a lot younger, but I'm sure that's her."

I took the photo and was surprised at how young Tasha looked.

"I thought you said she was young." I couldn't help but see the big smile on Mac's face.

"She is young." She snapped the photo out of my hands. "Hell, you're young compared to me."

"So she's my age?" I asked, putting pieces together. Harriette hummed out a yes. "I bet she and Mac went to college together. Richard said Mac was never at a loss for women." I stood there and contemplated whether I'd ever heard Richard mention a Tasha, but I didn't recall.

"Here we go." Harriette had opened a closet door and taken out a shoe box. "Lots of letters in here."

She brought the box over to the desk.

"Gosh, it seems so personal to look through these." I picked up the letters and cards. There were happy birthday cards. Always signed with big X's and O's. There were even some with lipstick kisses on them. I shuffled through them.

"Is there a return address?" I asked when I noticed none of them had envelopes.

"Just the cards and letters." Harriette was busy reading the letters. "I had no idea Mac was going to visit this woman so much."

"You should know," I said under my breath and put the cards I'd read back into the box. "I have another letter from her for today's delivery."

"What is the return address?" Harriette asked.

"There isn't one. Only a postmark from Tennessee. It's a broad city stamp that would cover miles of homes." I shrugged.

"This woman must've been married before. That's the woman I saw him fighting with." Harriette had found a photo at the bottom of the shoe box. The photo was of Tasha, Mac, and a little girl.

"I wonder if she got married after college and over the past few years had gotten divorced. He has been so worried about me and Grady that he didn't want to tell us." My stomach dropped, and I felt terrible. I'd been so wrapped up in my life and had not even thought about Mac and his needs. "He's always put everything on the line for me and Grady. This is why I have to find Tasha. According to Mac, he claims she won't be coming around anymore, but she's just our ticket to figuring this out and getting on the road to the real killer."

I held the photo in my grip and stared at it a little longer. Mac had always been good with Grady when he was little. I could only imagine how he'd been with Tasha's daughter. Tasha had shoulder-length brown hair and big brown eyes. Her daughter looked just like her.

"Are you going to ask him about it?" Harriette asked.

"No. I only want to find her first so he's got a solid alibi and witness. After she comes forward, I'll let him go and live his life." It was a vision I had to come to terms with. "Richard never left Mac in charge of his family."

"We all love you and Grady." Harriette put the cards and letter back in the box. "We need to put these back where we found them."

"Don't tell anyone we were in here, or Angela will arrest us for not only breaking and entering but also tampering with evidence," I told her.

"You talking about all those old coots?" She referred to the front porch ladies. "They can't hardly hear anything I tell them."

Harriette and I snuck back out of Mac's house. When she took a right into her gate, I quickly moved down Little Creek Road, delivering the mail as quickly as my legs would carry me.

"Hey, Buster." I flipped him a treat before he could start barking and wake up the neighbors. "How are you?" I asked him after he gobbled up the treat and came back to the fence for another one.

"You're early." Mr. Macum opened the door, scaring me half to death. "Thanks for the stamps yesterday."

"You're welcome." I handed him the junk mail. "I'm early because I'm trying to help out my friend Mac."

Then it dawned on me. I looked at Mr. Macum and twirled around to look at the bridge right across the street from his house.

"Mr. Macum, did you hear or see anything on Thursday night?" I asked.

"Nope. I keep to myself." He gave a hard nod.

"Yes. I understand that, but I don't know if you know, but yesterday…"

"You found that man's body." He must've seen the commotion. "I just like to keep to myself."

"Yes, but my friend Mac Tabor, your neighbor…"

"The man who is buying the country club to build all those condos? We've got enough traffic in this town as it is. We don't need any stinking condos and more people." He looked at the sign in his yard.

"Well, that's not what I was going to say, but you do have a point. Really, I just wanted to know if you saw anything funny or suspicious or heard a gunshot?" I asked. When I noticed he wasn't budging, I said, "My friend Mac's life depends on it. I don't think he did it, but he's going to be charged with murder."

"It's none of my business. I voted for Angela Hafley as sheriff, and I think she'll do a fine job of figuring out who killed that man." He patted his leg, and Buster came running up and into the house. "Have a good day. Don't catch a cold."

THIRTEEN

Between Mr. Macum not wanting to be of any help and my not finding Tasha's mailing address, it appeared my efforts on Little Creek Road had been futile.

I went back to Main Street, where I finished up the shops' deliveries. Iris did have a lot of outgoing mail, but she wasn't in, so I couldn't tell her about what Harriette and I had found out about all of Tasha's love letters.

I'd also decided not to return to Tabor Architects with the key. I figured I'd be able to disguise it in the mail on Monday, hoping they'd think they'd just overlooked it if they'd been looking for it.

"Good morning!" I sorted the diner's mail on the way through the door. I gave the bills to my dad and the junk to my mama. I sat down on the stool and put my mailbag on the floor. "How's it going?"

"We're all fine. Just fine." Mama looked over her shoulder. She cut a slice of her homemade Southern pecan butter bread, put it on a plate, and slapped some butter on top to melt. "How's Mac?" She set the plate in front of me. "You need to eat."

She didn't have to tell me twice. I didn't even bother using a fork; I just pinched off pieces and washed them down with a hot cup of coffee Mama also sat in front of me.

"I don't know. I didn't talk to him this morning." I took another sip.

"He went in early. I seen him with a coffee from the Roasted Bean, and shortly after, Julia ran out, saying something about fielding phone calls this morning." Mama leaned on the counter and folded her arms, eyeballing me to make sure I was going to eat all of the big slice of bread she had given me.

"I've been doing some digging around." I knew my mama wasn't going to like what I was doing.

"What? We try to keep things swept under the rug." She lifted a brow.

"I told Mac I'd keep my eyes and ears open to see if there are any rumblings about who else could possibly want to kill Chuck Shilling." I pinched off another piece of bread and stuck it in my mouth, letting the buttery goodness take over my senses. It was a much-needed stress relief.

"I like Mac. He's done good by you and my grandbaby." She leaned in a little more, topping off my coffee. It was her way of making me hang around a little longer. "Audrey came in, and she said she was actively looking for another job. I asked her why, figuring the country club would go off the market since Chuck was, well, you know, and thinking that his demise killed the deal." Mama shook her head. "Nope. She said the club was going to have to close because it was bankrupt and everyone is jumping ship. Including Kenneth Simpson. He hasn't showed up to any of his clients' golf lessons. They are demanding their money back."

"Did you give Audrey a job?" I asked, knowing Mama had been wanting to get out of the kitchen a little more. But when one owned a restaurant, it was a twenty-four-hour gig. I knew this well, because I had worked in the diner since I could walk.

"Thinking on it." She grabbed my empty plate.

"Thank you, that was good." I took another drink of my coffee and wiped my mouth. I picked up the now-much-lighter mailbag and stood up, tossing it over my shoulder. "I know you hear a lot of gossip, so let me know if you hear anything."

"As long as you don't do anything to get you in trouble." She gave me the Mom look, which proved one was never too old to get the Mom look.

"I won't." I gave her a hug. "I'll see you and Dad tomorrow night for supper," I reminded her before I headed to the General Store to get Vince's burner phone from Gill.

"Mornin'!" Gill lifted his head from the morning paper on the counter. "I got some mail for ya." Gill was a good ol' boy who wore overalls and boots. He was about my parents' age.

"I've got some for you too." I weaved in and out of the standing displays. "And I need one of those phones you add minutes to."

"Ahhh…" He lifted a brow. "Anyone I know?"

"Huh?"

"Most people come in here to get these phones to disguise who they are talking to." He reached behind him and took a phone off the hook before he rang it up.

I wasn't about to tell him it was for Vince and some FBI sleuthing, but I did want to know about the spray paint. "I'm looking for some information on spray paint. Has anyone come in to buy some?"

"Everyone who has a kid at Sugar Creek Gap High. They all came in here and bought all the brown, red, and gold paint to make all those signs for the game. Poor Ashley Williams was a little too late."

When he laughed, my ears perked up. Ashley Williams was the last person on my suspect list.

"Oh no. What happened?" I questioned, laying it on thick as if I really cared that poor Ashley didn't get the Grizzly colors. I took out my wallet and handed him the cash for the phone.

"Well, she said she was making some signs for the game, but the only color I had to give her was orange."

"Did you say she bought orange spray paint?" My gut dropped. Angela had said someone had spray-painted the country club with orange spray paint.

"She bought me out of that color too." He held the phone out to me. "Said it was the closest color to red we had and it'd be fine for what she was going to do with it."

"Thanks, Gill." I bounced on my toes. "You've been a big help."

He muttered something when I hurried out the door, but I didn't stay to hear it. Ashley Williams had not only spray-painted the country club to make it look like Mac did it, she'd framed him for murder!

FOURTEEN

"And how did Ashley get Mac's gun?" Angela crossed her arms and let out a deep sigh.

When I left the General Store, I went straight to the sheriff's department with the news about Ashley buying all the spray paint.

"I don't know that, but I do know Ashley bought Gill Tillett out of orange spray paint." I was handing her this information on a platter, but she wasn't too impressed.

She uncurled her arms and pushed herself off the edge of her desk, grabbing the phone behind her.

"Vita," Angela said to Vita Dickens, the dispatch operator for the department. "Can you send out a deputy to talk to Ashley Williams and question her about the orange spray paint she bought at the General Store?"

She let out a few ahs, huns, and hms before she hung up the phone. "Happy?" she asked me.

"Yes. Thank you." I nodded. "I understand Kenneth Simpson has an alibi. What about Dennis Kuntz?"

"Why, Bernadette Butler, if I didn't have this here badge resting on my chest, I'd've thought you were elected sheriff of Sugar Creek Gap." It was not only apparent in her tone but written all over her face that she didn't like my line of questioning.

"I'm really just trying to help out Mac." I thought she'd understand.

"He's got a lawyer for that. The best thing you can do for him is to be his friend." She said that as if there was some more evidence against Mac that I didn't know of. "Thank you for letting us know about the orange spray paint. We will check that out."

"Did you find any spray paint at Mac's house?" I asked before she pointed to the door.

My phone rang as I was leaving the department.

"Iris, I think Ashley might be the killer," I said in a hushed tone as I rushed past a group of reporters in the courthouse as I tried to get to the front door.

"Where are you?" she asked.

"I'm just leaving the courthouse and going to rush to deliver the rest of my route." I wrapped the scarf more tightly around my neck. The gray clouds had started to take over the day and bring a rush of cold air in with them.

"While I was delivering some pies today, all the talk was about the country club and Chuck. Someone told me they'd heard Ashley had cornered Chuck at Madame's." I nearly dropped the phone as she talked. "You come right over to Pie in the Face after your deliveries, and we'll go have a cocktail at Madame's."

Iris didn't have to say it out loud, but I knew she meant we were going to go see if anyone wanted to tell us anything.

"Yeah. I'll buy."

We said our goodbyes, and I headed to the east neighborhoods, where they had mailboxes on the street that made my job a lot easier.

Even though the temperature was getting cooler by the minute, the fast pace I was keeping actually was making me sweat.

"Are you okay?" Vince asked when I stopped by his condo to drop off the phone before meeting Iris.

"I'm fine. You aren't going to believe everything I found out today."

He ushered me in.

"Kenneth Simpson was out of town, and Ashley Williams is behind the country club spray-painting job."

He already knew.

"How?" I asked as I took the phone from my bag.

"I told you I had ways." He winked and took the phone. "I have a friend who likes to play golf. He lives on the thirteenth tee. I called him up and asked him to send me his Ring Doorbell footage. It showed her perfectly. I sent it to the sheriff, and she asked me if I'd talked to you."

We laughed.

"Yeah, she gave me a hard time after Gill told me Ashley bought the orange spray paint." I shook my head.

"I even had my buddy go over to Ashley's house and look in her garbage cans. Nothing, but..." A big smile crossed Vince's lips when he hesitated. "He went to the country club dumpster and found all the empty orange cans."

"That means Mac is cleared." I brought my hands up to my face. Tears stung my eyes.

"Only on the spray-paint charges." His news busted my bubble. "Unfortunately, Ashley lawyered up when the deputy brought her in. Some fancy attorney from somewhere else. He won't even be here until Monday."

"Are they holding her?" I questioned.

"It seems like they are for twenty-four hours." He shook his head. "I'm just not sure how she got Mac's gun."

That was the million-dollar question.

"For now, I think you need to keep looking into things. I'm still trying to get into the nursing home security system to see what time Dennis Kuntz left Thursday after visiting his mother. I'm a little rusty with all this new technology." He tapped his temple with his crooked finger. "I'll get it, though."

"Iris and I are going to Madame's, because Iris heard Ashley and Chuck had an argument there. So we are going to go and see if anyone heard them." I hiked the strap of the empty mailbag up on my shoulder.

"Let me get my coat." Vince turned around.

"You're not going," I told him.

"I told you this morning I've always wanted to get an Uber there, so I'm going."

He wasn't about to take no for an answer.

FIFTEEN

"And how did she rope you into this?" Iris was cleaning out the ovens at Pie in the Face, as she did every night before she went home.

Vince was busy shuffling in front of the bakery display case while licking his lips. "Pies, pies, and more pies." His eyes were glazed over. "These all look so good."

"I didn't rope him into anything." I moved around the counter. "Which one do you want?" I asked Vince.

He lifted his hand and pointed to the silk pie then shook his head and pointed to the lemon Philly pie.

"What if we give you a piece of each and you can take one home?" I smiled when his eyes lit up. "I'll pay," I said after I heard Iris give a little harrumph.

"I was the one who exposed Ashley Williams as the one who spray-painted the golf course." Vince took the plate with the slice of lemon Philly on it and sat down at one of the few café tables in the middle of the bakery. He left out the part about his FBI background and the people he knew.

"Do they think she killed Chuck? Because if they do, we don't need to go to Madame's." Iris made a good point. "Though I could use a drink." She made another good point, so we all agreed and helped her finish cleaning up.

Well, I helped her clean up. Vince only cleaned his plate. He didn't leave a single morsel of pie on it.

Madame's wasn't the kind of bar I'd ever step foot in. It wasn't that I was too good for it, but it was a rocker bar with loud jukebox rock-and-roll music. Give me a good old country song or even a pop song to bebop too and I was happy-go-lucky. This rock music and chicks in leather were not what I'd thought Mac was all about, but as I was finding out more and more, Mac was nothing like I'd thought he was.

Not only that, but it was smoky.

"I thought there was no more smoking in bars." I fanned my hand in front of my face, not only to catch a breath but to part the smoke so I could see.

"What can I get ya?" The burly man behind the bar had on a leather cap, a short-sleeved heavy-metal-band shirt, and a leather vest.

"We'll have three beers." I held up three fingers in hopes he was reading lips, because I could barely hear myself think above the blaring screams of the singer much less hear my own voice.

He must've understood me, because he came back with three bottles of beer, though I'd never said which kind. We didn't care. I played with a book of matches while the three of us sat there like bumps on a log.

"I've not seen a book of matches in years." Iris took one of the packs and slipped it into her purse.

"Me either." I looked at the logo of Madame's and ran my finger across it.

"So, why are you really here?" The bartender slung a couple of shots back while he waited for the three of us to answer. "It's not every day we see two middle-aged women and an old man come in here. We have regulars."

"We are looking for some answers." Iris was beating around the bush.

"Specifically this guy." I took my phone out and showed him a photo of Mac and Grady. "The guy on the right."

"Yeah. He was in here a few nights ago. What about him?" he asked.

"I'm a good friend of his and …"

"I'm not ratting the guy out if that's what you wanted to know." He waved his hands in front of him before he took the wet towel and wiped down the bar top.

"No. In fact, he's being accused of murder, and we're trying to find other suspects to help clear him."

I wasn't sure if he believed me.

"And we want to know if you saw this guy." Vince pulled out a newspaper clipping with Chuck's photo.

Iris and I looked at him, both thinking it was odd he'd brought a newspaper clipping.

"I'm old-school. Remember?" He laughed and set the piece of newspaper on the bar. "This is the guy Mac Tabor is accused of killing, and we think it was the girl with him that did it."

"Dude." The bartender nodded. "I saw this on the TV. I was wondering how I recognized his face. When you put both of their photos together, I remember." He continued to nod. "Yeah. They sat right over there." He pointed to the far end of the bar. "This lady with brown hair to here. Loud." He'd described Ashley to a T. "Yeah. Her and that guy got into a fight. They ended up leaving together."

"What about him?" I asked and showed him my phone again with Mac's photo.

"He left in an Uber way before them. He was smashed drunk." The bartender laughed. "I had to quit serving him. Dude was off the charts."

"Looks like we have some eyewitnesses here that say Ashley left with Chuck."

It was a great lead, and if the hour weren't so late, I would have called the department and had them come up here to talk to the bartender, but I figured Ashley was already in custody for twenty-four hours.

"Would you be willing to identify them to the Sugar Creek Gap sheriff?"

Vince took the whole sleuthing thing to a whole new level. I sat there in awe as he worked the young man into exactly what he wanted to.

By the time we'd finished our beers, Vince had gotten the guy to agree to meet him down at the department tomorrow afternoon after the bartender woke up.

"That was amazing." I gasped for air after we walked out.

"It was a cool place."

Iris was off her rocker.

"No, I meant how Vince handled that guy back there."
I rolled my eyes and got into Iris's passenger seat in the
back, giving the front to Vince.

"Just years of shaking people down." Vince took pride
in his former profession.

"Let's see what we've come up with." I pulled my
phone out and started to go back through my notes. "We
can cross Kenneth Simpson off the list because he's got a
solid alibi, being out of town on an interview, along with
Tim Crouse's statement."

I used the back button to erase Kenneth from my notes.

"Poor Mac. I still can't explain how someone got his
gun unless Ashley slipped in there." I frowned when I
realized I couldn't technically take him off the list, but even
deeper was the hurt that I truly felt that I didn't know the
real Mac Tabor.

"Dennis Kuntz?" I questioned Vince.

"Yep. I got the footage. I even went to the night-shift
nurses' station to ask to make sure I was right." Vince
turned his chin slightly to the left as he spoke so I could
hear him. "He fell asleep at his mom's on Thursday night,
and when he woke up, it was too late to go home, so he
stayed there. Video cameras show it, so he's off the list."

"That leaves Ashley Williams, who has motive because she lives in the neighborhood and wants the best for her daughter. I'd kill for Grady." It was a sad but true statement. A mother's love would go up against practically anything. "And if that wasn't enough, she tried to set Mac up for the spray-painting, she verbally threatened him in public, and she was seen leaving with Chuck right before he was murdered."

"Leading him back to Little Creek Road so it looked like Mac did it." Iris smacked the steering wheel with the heel of her hand. "If Mac was as hammered as the bartender said, do you think Ashley could've gone in his house and taken the gun?"

"She shot Chuck on the bridge. He fell over and then she tossed the gun in the bushes after she cleaned it off." Vince finished up the theory.

I typed away in my notes under her name.

"All of this could be possible." I nodded. "I'll send these notes to your phone in a text so you can give them to Angela."

"You don't want to meet us down there?" Vince asked.

Iris was pulling up to his condo.

"I've got a full day off work, and I plan to clean and cook for my family," I told him before he got out. "But let me know what happens."

"Oh, I will." He bent down into the car. "You know what, I hate how someone died, but I have to say that I've had a lot of fun dipping my toe back into the investigation work."

"I hope all this work is to help Mac out and not hurt him worse." I couldn't help but think all the snooping we'd done here and there was for nothing.

SIXTEEN

I wasn't sure if it was the relief I felt after the bartender had identified Ashley not only arguing with Chuck but leaving the bar with him that I had a sense of peace that all was going to be good for Mac. But the last thing I remembered was snuggling Rowena on the couch with my phone in hand so I could call Mac to tell him what we had found out.

It wasn't until Rowena had practically smacked me awake to feed her that I realized it was morning.

Instead of calling and giving Mac the good news, I simply included him in the family text that I was going to be cooking our favorite shrimp-and-sausage gumbo for supper and to be here by five p.m.

With a few cups of coffee down me and a nice hot shower, I ran to the grocery store and picked up the hot sausage, shrimp, crushed tomatoes, tomato sauce, onions, okra, and frozen vegetables along with a couple of bags of rice. Of course, I had to make my famous cheesecake-stuffed pumpkin bread, too. It was Mac's favorite, and I was seeing our supper as a little celebration of his not being a murder suspect.

I'd leave all the questions I had about his relationship with Tasha for another day. Today was a time to celebrate, because according to Vince's burner-phone text message, he and the bartender were on their way to the sheriff's department.

I pulled the truck into my driveway and pulled a little too hard on the paper bag, ripping the bottom out of it. I reached down to the floorboard and grabbed my empty mailbag and threw the groceries in it, carefully balancing the other paper sacks so it didn't tear apart.

"Hello, Rowena," I greeted my little girl, practically tripping over her as she rubbed against me. "Let me get these groceries put away, and we will play."

Since I was gone all day long, I really did try to spend as much time as possible playing with Rowena on the weekends. She loved the little feather-on-a-stick toy the ladies at the nursing home had made during one of their crafting classes.

I took the food out of the mailbag first, because the last thing I needed was a stinky mailbag tomorrow.

"What is that?" I reached the bottom of the bag and noticed a letter. "Mac," I groaned when I realized it was the letter from Tasha I was supposed to deliver when I decided to break and enter instead. "Well, he won't realize the date." I put it back in the mailbag to deliver with tomorrow's mail.

The letter kept coming back into my brain as my eyes focused on the bag lying on my kitchen table.

"No. We can't look," I told Rowena as if she was going to agree with me. "It's not our mail."

She jumped up on the table and lay on my bag as if she was telling me to open it.

"No. It's illegal, and I could get fired." I looked at her eyes. "I know. No one would know. Tasha would think it got lost in the mail." I flung the sausage back and forth as I reasoned it out, finally putting it in the refrigerator.

Rowena let out a little meow as if she agreed.

"And it's not like the other letters she sent had anything in them." I didn't really recall any important information other than that she loved him and couldn't wait to be together. "Is it?"

Rowena stretched out. I stood there, gnawing the inside of my cheek, before I shooed her off the table.

Before I even knew what I was doing, it was like the devil dove inside me, and I ripped that letter open.

"Mac, I won't be ignored," I read out loud to Rowena. "Did you hear that? She won't be ignored." I read it so dramatically Rowena took special interest and sat up. "If you don't come through with the money, I'll be forced to tell everyone your big dark secret and then what will you do? Poor, poor you. Ellie will hate you. Can you live with that? If you don't come by my house on Sunday, you can kiss everything about your secret little life goodbye."

I blinked.

"She's sending death threats through the postal service, Rowena. This is illegal." I shook the letter. "This is my new address. Be there. I'm not kidding."

I eased down into the kitchen chair and put the letter on the table.

"Seriously." I ran my hand down Rowena's back. "Do you think Mac killed Chuck? How much money are we talking here?"

My mind reeled for about five minutes as I noodled what to do.

"I think I'm going to go talk to her. Woman to woman." I nodded at Rowena and grabbed my keys to the truck. "I'll be back in time to fix supper."

I didn't tell her Mac might not be there, depending on what I found out from Tasha. It would crush Rowena's furry little heart.

If I timed it just right by my phone GPS, I could get to Tasha's house across the Tennessee line in about an hour, visit with her for an hour, and then be back on the road in plenty of time.

The only thing I didn't factor in was all those Tennessee mountains and how my GPS didn't like them.

"Hi." I stopped at the next gas station and took the letter with the address of Tasha Linder with me to show to the attendant. "Do you know this address?" I asked the girl behind the counter.

"Ms. Linder." She nodded and smiled. "Why?"

"Oh good, you do know her." I put my hand up to my heart and pretended I was glad, though I really wanted to know what her big secret with Mac was. "I'm a long-time friend of hers from college." I made sure I threw that in there because it was how Mac said he'd met her. "And we recently connected on Facebook, of all places, after all these years," I lied. "And she gave me her address." I flipped the letter over and showed her the address. "My GPS on my phone is having the hardest time finding her house in these mountains."

The girl took a long look at the scribbled address. She hesitated.

"Can you point me in the right direction?" I put my hands together in a "pretty please" way.

"I…" She hesitated again. "Sure. You're gonna go out of the gas station right. Then the second left you're gonna drive down this windy road until you come to a fork. There's an old, run-down barn on the right. It's got a red door. You ain't gonna miss it. Go the opposite direction. Then you're gonna come to a real old church with a big white steeple. Keep going past that until you see a bunch of donkeys on the left. Turn there." My head was spinning with her directions. I grabbed the pen next to the cash register and tried to write down and remember the landmarks.

"You're gonna go up a big hill like a mountain, and there's going to be a big steel gatehouse on the right. That's not hers. Hers is the little cabin directly across from it.

There's an old blue Chevy Nova on cement blocks. That's how you'll know it's her house."

"Thank you so much." I smiled at the girl. "I truly appreciate it." I couldn't get out of there fast enough.

"Ma'am." The girl stopped me when I turned around.

"Yes." I answered without looking back at her.

"My pen."

A sigh of relief waved through my body when I realized it was only the pen she wanted back and not to question me any more about Tasha.

"Yes." I held it up and slapped it onto the counter. "Thank you."

I hurried out the store and jumped into the truck.

I drove the truck in and out of those curves, making sure to keep repeating the landmarks as I came to them.

"Opposite direction," I read out loud when I'd gotten to the fork in the road with the red-doored barn.

The closer up the mountain to Tasha's house I got, the faster my heart raced. There was a big secret between her and Mac that I needed to know, and maybe she'd be able to provide some sort of information to help me prove Mac didn't kill Chuck. If Mac said he was with Tasha, I needed to get her to prove it even if Angela wasn't making a great effort to do so.

When I pulled in, Tasha was just getting out of her car.

"Well, you aren't Mac." Tasha stood at the door. In one hand, she had a rolled-up McDonald's sack, and with the other, she was gripping a little girl's hand. "Let me introduce you to my and Richard's daughter, Ellie."

Richard's daughter. My mouth dried. My heart raced. Then a little bit of panic set in.

"Ellie, this is Mac's friend." Tasha didn't refer to me as Richard's wife. She opened the front door, and they walked in. "Are you coming?"

I gulped and, against my intuition, went in.

"She and I have a little bit of business to discuss. Can you run over to the Basses' and see if they have some sugar we can borrow for those brownies we are going to make for school tomorrow? You can eat along the way." Tasha handed the food sack to the little girl.

"Nice to meet you, ma'am."

The little girl looked at me, and instantly I tried to find Richard in her but didn't. My heart sank to my feet.

"I might be a minute." Ellie bounced up on her toes and kissed her mom. "I want to pet their new puppies."

"That's fine. Just be home by ten."

When Tasha said that, I knew she wasn't planning on baking any sort of brownies for school tomorrow. I looked at the clock on the wall next to the door. It made me nervous, because ten p.m. was a long ways away.

The door closed behind the little girl. Tasha put her hand up for me not to move. She peeled back the curtain from the window and peered out. I could see the little girl skipping across the street to the large steel gate.

"Now, we have some business to take care of." She reached over and dropped her keys in the basket on the table beside the door. She slid open the drawer.

"I was just coming by to ask if you'd please help me with Mac's release for being accused of..." My jaw clenched, and my eyes focused on the gun in her hand. "Listen, I had no idea Richard..."

"Are you stupid or something?" She waved the gun in front of her. "You think Richard had been coming to Tennessee every week on business? No." She shook her head. "I met him years ago when a group of my friends and I went to a bar. Oh, he *was* on business. Then he made *me* his business."

"Are you telling me Richard had a relationship with you?" My head was so jumbled I couldn't figure out if he'd had a one-night stand or a relationship, because she sure did sound like they'd had a relationship.

Was I to believe her?

"Please, put that gun away. You're scaring me." I started to realize there was more to this story than I knew.

"Chuck Shilling overheard me and Mac arguing about money and Richard." She waved the gun around all willy-nilly.

"Money?"

"Ellie deserves a life. Her daddy died." She tapped the gun to her chest. "My Richard died, leaving us with nothing. I've worked hard over the past ten years to become the manager of Food City. It's taken every bit of Richard's inheritance and what I make to make ends meet."

"Inheritance?" I questioned then realized that all those letters Mac had been getting from the Tennessee address were actually to Richard. I bet Mac was giving them to Richard, and Richard was storing them at Mac's. Mac's financial problem was Tasha and Ellie, Richard's problem.

"First Federal every month puts in a lump sum of money in Ellie's name. Only it stopped about three months ago. I started writing Mac since I didn't have his phone number, and he refused to answer me. I even sent him a photo of Ellie, begging him to help us out and find out where the money had gone." Tasha's black eyes narrowed.

It was then that I noticed her hair was cut exactly like Ashley Williams's. The bartender had had it right. We'd had it wrong.

"Come to find out, Mac had been putting money into an account so you and your little boy wouldn't find out about us after Richard died," her sordid tale continued.

Then it hit me.

"Richard paid for two families?" I just couldn't believe what I was hearing. This would kill Grady.

"You want to know how angry I was that night? I had to find a babysitter for Ellie so I could drive to Sugar Creek Gap to find Mac. Then Chuck Shilling showed up."

She'd already told me this, which made me think she was getting nervous and jumbling her thoughts.

"I didn't know about you so why are you going to hurt me?" Not that she'd hurt me yet, but judging by the situation, she looked as if she was going to.

"Because you know!" she screamed. "And don't play dumb with me!"

"Okay, so I know." I didn't have a clue what she was talking about.

"You think I can just let you leave here and go back to that nosy sheriff of yours and tell her Richard had a love child? She'd for sure connect the dots that I was the one who killed that old man."

My mouth went dry.

"You killed Chuck?" I choked out. My eyes shifted back and forth as I tried to add this little nugget to all the other jumbled-up pieces in my head. "Why?"

"You are an idiot. I just told you he overheard me and Mac arguing about the money." She held up her free hand and rubbed the pads of her fingers and thumb together. "He was at Mac's house discussing this big business venture. I busted in and started going off about the money from Richard stopping."

"Let me guess." I frowned, and tears welled in my eyes. "Chuck figured out Richard had a child by you, Mac had been paying you to make it look like Richard had been, and he told Mac that if Mac didn't drop buying the property, then he was going to expose Richard. All because he didn't want Mac to turn around and sell the condos, giving you the money for Ellie to live on." I blinked, and the tears fell. "Mac didn't want Richard to look bad in the community, so they had a fight. He kicked Chuck out..."

"He kicked Chuck out and then me. He said he had to think about it and that I should give him until the morning. But it wasn't Richard he was trying to protect." The disgust was written all over her face. "It was you."

"Me?"

"Come on," she snarled. "Richard even told me how Mac had a thing for this lady who had a kid and lived on a farm. Richard described you to a T, but the catch was that she was married. I had no idea he was talking about his own wife." She was saying things I didn't want to hear. "So I followed Chuck to a local bar. Got him all good and drunk, because I told Mac before I left his house that he was going to build those condos and give me a couple for income.

"Mac was good and liquored up. I put him in an Uber, figuring I could talk Chuck into selling the country club, and when he wasn't budging, I worked my magic on him. I knew exactly where Mac kept his gun, and it was easy to hit on old Chuck, making him think he was going to get a little." She was enjoying every second of this.

I was having a hard time catching my breath. I bent over and placed my hands on my knees.

"Lord, you're gonna keel over, and I'm not going to have to kill you myself." Her tone told me she was pretty pleased with the reaction I was having.

Only…

I knew this feeling all too well. The first time I'd had it was when Richard and I took Grady on his first vacation to Florida. We drove over a long bridge across the bay to get to our hotel. I could hardly breathe driving over the bridge in fear we were going to plunge to our deaths. It was my first panic attack. There were a few more here and there, but nothing like the one I'd had when I was told Richard was dead.

"Please just give me some water before you let me die here." I gasped and eased myself down onto a chair before I truly did pass out.

"I've never heard of anyone coming out of a heart attack with a drink of water." She shrugged.

With blurry vision, I watched as she went into her kitchen.

My chest heaved as I tried to take deep breaths and get myself out of this panic attack. It was as if nothing was real around me, but I knew if I could think of something I might get out of this situation.

That's a blue couch. That's a blue couch. That's a blue rug. I repeated the things I saw that were blue. I'd had enough therapy to learn that when I was having a panic attack, if I focused on something that was real, like a color, I was able to distinguish that the feelings caused by the panic attack weren't real.

Just as I heard her turn off the water faucet, I looked behind me to see if there was a weapon or fireplace poker or something. There was a baton. It had to be Ellie's. It wasn't one of the full-sized ones but a smaller one.

Slowly, I dragged it over to me and slid it under my thigh.

"Please call the ambulance," I begged Tasha for good measure, though I was feeling much better.

As she got closer, I noticed the gun wasn't in her hands. I figured she'd put it down in the kitchen, possibly thinking she didn't need it because I was dying of what she thought was a heart attack.

Think again.

With a shaky hand, I reached up to get the water at the same time I gripped the baton under my leg and swung it up to meet Tasha's skull.

I jumped up, dropping the glass, and watched her go down in slow motion.

She didn't move. She was knocked out cold.

I ran over to the door where I'd seen the shoes and jump rope. I knew I had to get her tied up so I could call 9-1-1.

With her bound by the jump rope, I walked to the kitchen, where I found the gun. I pulled my phone out of my pocket and dialed 9-1-1, picking up the gun with the phone tucked in between my shoulder and ear.

"Yes. Please, I need help. Someone has tried to kill me." I rattled off the address.

Exhausted.

I slid down the door with the gun pointed at Tasha until I heard sirens barreling up through the mountains.

"Bernie! Where are you?"

I jumped up when I heard Mac calling my name. I jerked the door open.

"Mac!" I dropped the gun and ran into his open arms. I was mad at him for keeping Richard's secret, but I was so glad to see him.

Sheriff Angela Hafley appeared out of nowhere. "Where is she?"

"Inside."

I looked around and noticed Angela's sheriff car. Confused, I looked back at Mac. "How did you find me?"

"Mr. Macum of all people." Mac smiled and dragged me back into his arms, running his hand down my hair. "He saw someone who looked a whole lot like Tasha on the bridge with Chuck. He said both of them looked drunk and as if they were having a lovers' quarrel. Buster was barking the whole time they were fighting. He said he'd not paid any attention to it until you mentioned it to him when you were delivering his mail. He has one of the Ring Doorbells and looked back at the footage. As soon as Tasha shot him, Buster barked, but Mr. Macum doesn't hear very well and he'd just taken off his hearing aids."

I smiled. Tears of relief rolled down my face.

Another Sheriff cruiser and an ambulance pulled up. The first responders ran into the house. Angela walked outside and talked to the officer.

"When you weren't home for Sunday supper, everyone knew something was wrong. I went to the sheriff's department to report you missing. Angela is the one who asked me if she thought Tasha might have you, but I had no idea where she moved." He drew back and looked down at me. Tears clung to his bottom eyelids.

"Uncle Mac?" Ellie was standing behind us with the neighbor. "What is going on with Mommy?"

Mac looked at me and then back to Ellie. He dropped his arms from around me and walked over to kneel in front of her.

"She's okay, Ellie Belly." He reached out and tickled her stomach.

"Why don't we go back to my house, and you stay the night until your mommy feels better." The neighbor and Mac looked at each other.

"Yeah. That's a great idea." Mac planted a big grin on his face for the little girl and nodded.

"A sleepover?" Ellie was innocent in this entire mess and had no idea what was going on.

"Yeah. A sleepover." The neighbor grabbed Ellie by the hand.

"Bye, Uncle Mac." Ellie waved and went with the neighbor.

"I guess you know about Ellie now." Mac's big smile was long gone. "I'm not sure she's Richard's, but Tasha claimed she is."

"So this was Richard's Tennessee business?" I could hardly believe I was saying these words.

"He and Tasha had been together a really long time. They met when he came to see me, and I'm sorry." His voice cracked. "I'm so sorry. I tried to tell Richard..."

"I don't want to hear any more excuses." I watched Ellie cross the street. My heart broke for that little girl. "Her dad is dead, and now her mother will go to prison for murder."

"Tasha has a long history of telling lies to keep Richard. They'd not seen each other for a few months because Richard tried to break it off." As Mac told me about Richard's affair, I did recall that a few months before he died, he was home more than he'd ever been. "She told Richard she was pregnant with his baby. He was sick over it. Richard had set me up with an account to make sure money was funneled weekly to Tasha. When he died, I should've come clean, but I took over his payments and kept giving her money. I'm not even sure if Ellie is his kid."

"The business plan for the condos." I gasped. "The debt you owed was to Tasha."

It was becoming very clear the steps Mac took to make sure he kept Richard's secret.

"Yeah. She was going to tell you and Grady. I just couldn't do that."

"Richard didn't deserve you as a friend." I was so mad the tears poured out.

"No. Not Richard. You. I couldn't do that to you." His eyes searched my face. "Richard didn't deserve you. Tasha put a strain on our relationship. You. You." He gulped. "Bernadette, if you've not noticed, I've been single since the day I met you."

"What are you trying to say?" I blinked past the tears.

"I've been single all these years because no woman has ever been able to stand up against how I feel about you." He cupped his hand around my face and used the pads of his thumbs to wipe away my tears. "Richard knew I've been in love with you since the day you two started dating."

I blinked, trying to process what I was hearing.

"Did you think I really wanted to take the country club? It was the only land available for me to make money on and pay Tasha to keep her mouth shut. Madame's? Do you honestly think I'd go there? No. Tasha likes hard rock, and it was to keep her mouth shut." His hands slid from my face to my arms. "Can't you see that it was all for you?"

He pulled me to him. I melted into his body as he brought his lips to mine and sealed his words with a kiss that sent an electric shock wave to my tiptoes.

"I've seen it all now." Angela walked past with Tasha Linder in handcuffs, taking her to her car. "Mac Tabor saved the country club, solved a murder, and stole Widow Butler's heart all in one day." She snickered. "We got someone to drive your truck back to Sugar Creek Gap, Bernadette."

I was glad Angela knew I was in no shape to drive.

"Saved the country club?" I questioned Mac.

"Yeah. I figured I might as well put the money into the country club restaurant and pool instead of tearing everything down just to build some condos."

I started to see a glimpse of the old Mac I had known just two days ago—the real Mac Tabor.

"Ashley Williams agreed she'd get the city council to help the neighbors pass a homeowners' association fee so we won't be in this mess again."

"Widow Butler? Is that what people call me?"

"Not anymore if I can help it." Mac wrapped his arm around me and walked me to his car, and I knew he was going to take me home. "Let's get you home so you can make that gumbo for all the folks waiting at your house."

The entire way home, I stared out the window. I wasn't sure what my future with Mac was, and I wasn't sure how I was going to tell Grady he might have a little sister, but there was one thing I knew for sure.

Mac had been right. There was a houseful of people who loved me and were waiting for me when I got home. And I couldn't wait to get there into their warm embrace, exactly where I belonged.

OUT NOW FROM ADDISON MOORE &
BELLAMY BLOOM

Hello all! Have you checked out the new series by friend Addison Moore and her partner in cozy crime, Bellamy Bloom? It's a cute but deadly new series that centers around a mind reading innkeeper. The best part? The innkeeper can talk to animals. Fun! Be sure to grab a copy of Kittyzen's Arrest (Country Cottage Mysteries 1), it's a killer read.

https://www.amazon.com/Kittyzens-Arrest-Country-Cottage-Mysteries-ebook/dp/B07TP2BYY7

A little about the book:

An innkeeper who reads minds. An ornery detective. And a trail of bodies. Cider Cove is the premiere destination for murder.

My name is Bizzy Baker, and I can read minds. Not every mind, not every *time*, but most of the time, and believe me when I say it's not all it's cracked up to be.

*Bizzy Baker runs the Country Cottage Inn, has the ability to pry into the darkest recesses of both the human and animal mind, and has just stumbled upon a body. With the help of her kitten, Fish, a mutt named Sherlock Bones, and an ornery yet dangerously good-looking homicide detective, Bizzy is determined to find the killer.

Cider Cove, Maine is the premier destination for fun and relaxation. But when a body turns up, it's the premier destination for murder.

SNEAK PEEK-
HOLIDAY ROAST MORTEM
Book 7 in the Killer Coffee Mystery Series

ONE

The twinkling Christmas lights wrapped around the wooded deck of the Watershed Restaurant, sparkling on Lake Honey Springs and a nice romantic evening with Patrick was exactly what I needed to get into the spirit of season.

I'd been working so many long hours at The Bean Hive, my local coffee house, getting all the holiday coffee blends and baked sweet treats that were ordered by my customers ready that I'd not taken a lot of time for my relationship with my husband or our fur babies, Pepper and Sassy.

Pepper was a Schnauzer who found me when I went to I went to Pet Palace, our local SPCA, to find a roommate. It took me a second to look into his eyes and he stole my heart.

Pepper and Sassy went to work with me on a daily basis, but it wasn't the quality snuggles I was used to or they liked getting.

"You look beautiful." Patrick Cane reached over and laid his hand on mine. "I'm glad we made time for me and you."

"Me too." I put my other hand on top of his and rubbed it.

He owned Cane Construction and the economy had been booming around our small town of Honey Springs, Kentucky that he was just as busy as I had been at the coffee house.

Neither of us were complaining because we certainly had seasons of dry spells where the money just trickled in.

Patrick's big brown eyes and tender smile along with his sensitive heart was what drew me into when we were just teenagers and I would come to Honey Springs during the summers to visit my aunt.

It wasn't until years later, a law degree, a divorce under my belt and opening a coffee house that Patrick and I were reacquainted and now married. Practically perfect.

"Geez, buddy!" The man sitting next to us jumped up when the waiter accidentally knocked their table and spilled the man's water in his lap. "Watch what you're doing."

"Calm down, Ryan," the woman across from him had turned red. She looked around the restaurant to see if anyone was watching.

"Are you joking?" Ryan glared over at her. The poor waiter looked to be a busboy and he quickly replaced the man's glass with more water and apologized before walking away.

"No I'm not joking," she spat. "You can be such a jerk. Things happen."

The man grabbed the glass and took a drink, glaring at the woman across from him before he went back to finishing his meal.

"That looks delicious." Patrick and I pulled back our hands so Fiona Rosone, our waitress, could put our plates on the table, taking the attention off the couple next to us

Patrick's loving gaze had turned from me to the honey glazed salmon on his plate.

I had gotten the panko encrusted chicken, one of the Watershed's specials along with a sweet potato and asparagus. I would definitely be taking some of the sweet potato home with me to the dogs. Not only did they love it, but sweet potato was good for their digestion and their coat.

Since they came to work with me, I tried to keep an eye on them so customers wouldn't slip them something they'd ordered from the counter, but it was hard to police that. Plus, Pepper was a wonderful vacuum and sniffed out any little morsel of food.

"The babies?" Patrick's smile light up his face.

"Of course." I shrugged knowing how much I treated them like real human babies. Though having children were something Patrick and I did want, it just wasn't in the foreseeable future.

We'd only been married a year and the night of our honeymoon, my Aunt Maxine Bloom along with my mother, , started in on dropping hints about a bundle of joy.

"It's so pretty here tonight." I looked out the window of the floating restaurant. The Christmas tree on the outside deck was glowing with colored lights and fun ornaments that were lake themed. The Christmas trees inside of the Watershed was decorated a little more elegant with white lights and fancy ornamental ornaments, large ribbons, and bows. There was a sign sitting on a fancy gold stand with

Logsdon Landscaping Co. being recognized as the decorator.

Amy Logsdon had taken over the family landscaping business and when she did, she saw a need for people's help in decorating for all the seasons because we did celebrate every holiday on the calendar and decorated for them. We even just had our annual * festival in the town square last weekend. But what Amy did was amazing. She took the landscaping business to a whole 'nuther level. She take clients, like the Watershed, and completely decorates the entire outside of buildings and inside of them. This part of Logsdon Landscaping focus primarily on the outside decorations. Some people have hired the company to come to their homes and put up their lights, their large yard displays and more.

It really did help cut back on all the work the beautification committee had to do and frees up their time to focus on more of the business side of the festivals.

It's a very nice option to have, but I love to decorate and had made it part of my life to help me get so excited for the holidays.

They had beautiful views of the lake from their tables and they also did dinner cruises. The prices were steep and it was only special occasions that brought us there to eat. Spending some quality time with Patrick definitely was a special occasion.

"Is it?" Patrick looked over the candlelight at me. "I only notice how pretty you are."

"We are already married. You can stop laying it on thick." Fiona knew us so well, she'd already brought a to-go box over to the table for me to put in the dog's portion for me to take home.

"That was so good." Patrick pulled his wallet out of his pocket and took out the cash for the bill and leaned back in his chair. "Now we can go home, snuggle with the kids by the fire."

"Heaven." Sometimes I couldn't believe how I'd hit the jackpot in my thirties. In my twenties, it was a bumpy ride, but worth every up and down it took to get to this moment right here.

Both of us smiled at each other before another couple next interrupted with their loud argument.

"I told you that I've had it." The woman pointed her the steak knife at the man. "I won't put up with this behavior anymore."

"Keep your voice down," the man shushed her. "When we got married, you knew exactly what you were getting into."

"I've had enough." She picked her napkin up from her lap and wiped her mouth. "After Christmas, I'm filing for divorce."

"Over my dead body." He threw is napkin on his plate.

"So be it." She slammed her napkin on the table, the water splashed out of her glass.

The scoots of their chairs did cause others to look around, but since they were next to me and Patrick, I think we were the only ones who heard them arguing.

Patrick and I watched the couple rush out of the restaurant.

"I hope we don't ever get like that when we reach their age." Their sadness gnawed in my gut and I couldn't help but wonder if they were all goo-goo eyed like Patrick and I were.

"Never. Ever." He shook his head. "Unless Penny and Maxi stop getting along, then we might have a problem," he joked.

"I wouldn't be joking about them because they've already had a fallen out this week about who was going to bring the fruit cake to Christmas." I let out a long sigh.

"You decide." Patrick thought it was as easy as that when it clearly wasn't.

You see, my mom, Penny Bloom and my Aunt Maxine Bloom had never gotten along in my entire life, until recently. My mom had been really jealous of my relationship with my Aunt Maxi. And well…let's just say that I've always had a connection with my Aunt Maxi I'd never had with my mom and when I got divorced, it was obviously Aunt Maxi I'd run to. Here we were a few years later and some history under my belt, my mom had moved to Honey Springs. They were the reason Patrick and I were married by the Justice of the Peace.

"I've got enough people to coordinate besides refereeing them." I was now rethinking my decision to host a big Christmas supper for my friends and family at the Bean Hive Coffee Shop.

My friends and I had become family in our small community and I wanted to be surrounded by them during the holidays. Everyone has something special to bring to the occasion and it's going to be a joyous one even if mom and Aunt Maxi decide to not get along.

"Will that be all?" Fiona asked and picked up the check with the cash.

"Yes. Very good." Patrick pointed to the money. "Keep the change."

"Delicious as always." It was a treat to come to the Watershed and took some effort to actually get dressed, put on makeup and look presentable. Not like when I went to work at the coffee house with my hair pulled up, baking clothes on underneath my Bean Hive apron.

Patrick, being the southern gentleman he was, got up from his chair and walked over to help me out of mine.

"Let's get home and we can talk about grabbing one of the trees from the tree farm tomorrow." Patrick was speaking my language and he knew it.

"Fire, snuggles, decorating." I took his hand in mine. "Patrick Cane, you are something else."

"I just want to keep you happy during this Christmas get together." We walked toward the back of the restaurant so we could walk outside to look at the decorations. "I know how stressed you can get and if I can help out, I'm going to. So you," he opened the door to the outside and had me walk past him, "my dear, will be pampered by me."

He pulled me to him once the door shut behind us and shield me from the winter night wind as it whipped across the lake and over us, sending chills along my body.

Patrick stood behind me with his arms wrapped around me and we looked across the lake the Bee Farm where Kayla and Andrew Noro had big wood cut outs of bees with Santa hats on them all light up so the people on the land side of the lake could see them.

The Bee Farm was a small island in the middle of the lake. It was amazing to visit and see exactly how the bee farm did work. I got all my honey from Kayla. It was so fresh and tasty not only in the coffees and teas I served at The Bean Hive but also the baked goods.

"Everyone seems to be really ready for this season compared to last year," Patrick's warm breath tickled my ear. He rested his chin on my shoulder.

"Why did you mention that?" I jerked around and looked at him. "You are giving us bad ju-ju."

Last year we had a murder in Honey Springs at Christmas. Something I wanted to forget forever.

"It's not bad ju-ju." He laughed and grabbed my hand. "Let's get home to the kids."

We walked along the Watershed's pier toward the parking lot when we heard that same couple from inside the restaurant arguing outside near their truck.

"I'm telling you that I'm not going to stand for this. Do you understand?" Ryan yelled at the woman, who I assumed was his wife sense he'd said something about how she knew before they got married this was how it was.

"You know what." The woman jerked the door open. "I'm going to call a lawyer!"

The couple both slammed their doors. The tires squealed as their truck took off.

Patrick's grip tightened on my hand.

"I don't think they are going to have a good Christmas." He opened the passenger side door for me.

"Don't worry." I kissed him before I got in. "It took me a divorce to find you, I'm for sure not going to let you go."

I hooked my seatbelt while he got inside the car and started it up.

"The Logsdon Landscape really had done a fantastic job." Watershed was on one far left side of the boardwalk as we drove back to our cabin, passing by the entire pier where The Bean Hive was located.

The coffee house had a perfect location right in the middle of all the shops. Directly in front of the coffee house was a long pier that jutted out and perfect for people who liked to fish deeper out into the water.

"I love how they put the lighted garland around all the carriage posts," Patrick said about all the lights along the boardwalk. "It's prettier than just the wreaths."

"Yes, but the beautification committee did the best they could." I still had to give * credit. She did work hard on trying to make Honey Springs gorgeous during the festive times of the year. "It's so pretty."

Our cabin was located about a seven minute drive from the boardwalk. It was a very windy road running along the lake. I usually drove my bike with Pepper nestled in the front basket while Sassy went to work with Patrick at the construction sites for most of the day until he'd stop in for a cup of coffee. That's when she liked to stay at the coffee house with me and Pepper.

Lately, it'd been too cold or there was too much ice on the road to ride the bike.

"Be careful." I warned Patrick when he took one of the sharper curves. "There's black ice on the road."

The taillights of a truck in the distance started to cross over the center line of the small road.

"There must be some up there." Patrick pointed to the car. We watched as the driver jerked the truck back over. "Whoa!"

"Oh no!" I yelled as we watched the truck cross over again, this time going through the trees and down the embankment toward the lake.

I eased up in the seat of Patrick's truck and looked down to see if the people in the truck were okay when we got to the place they'd went off the road.

"Call 9-1-1!" Patrick yelled at me and put his truck in park when we saw the other truck had actually gone into the Lake Honey Springs and the front end was going under the water.

I fumbled for my phone and dialed all while trying to see Patrick through the pitch dark of night. The headlights of the sunken truck was fading fast into the depths of the water.

I rattled off the information to dispatch operator and jumped out of the car when I saw Patrick had jumped into the lake. I grabbed the blankets and his work flashlight out from behind the seats and headed down to the lake.

"Patrick!" I screamed when I didn't see him come back up from the frigid water. "Patrick!" I frantically screamed, dropping the blankets and shining the flashlight in the water. "Patrick!"

I ran up and down where the truck had gone in but not sure where it was because the headlights of the truck were no longer visible. When I heard some splashing a few yards out in the lake, I moved the flashlight and saw Patrick.

"I've got the woman!" Patrick swam toward the bank with the woman in the crock of his arm. "She's alive!"

In the distance, I could hear the sirens. They echoed off the lake. I ran to meet Patrick and the woman with one of the blankets to wrap around her.

"I've got to go and get the driver." He laid her gently on her side on the ground before he went right back into the water.

"Here," I told her, wrapping more blankets around her. "Are you okay?" I asked and when she looked up at me, I recognized her as the woman arguing with her husband in the Watershed.

"My husband," she tried to talk but was shivering. "My husband!" she jumped up as the shock of it all started to set in. "Ryan!" She screamed.

"Please, put this around you until the ambulance gets here." I tried to put the blanket back on her shoulders but she was trying to run back into the water. "Stop! Don't go back in there!"

"Ryan!" It was all she seemed to say while I jerked her back. Literally held her back.

The ambulance and police showed up, taking over just as Patrick had come back up from the depths of the Lake Honey Springs with the limp man over his shoulder.

After Patrick got him to shore, we let the emergency crew take over.

"What happened?" Sheriff Spencer Shepard asked when he got there.

"I think they hit black ice because we saw them swerve, then correct, then swerve again, ending up in the lake," Patrick told Spencer while we stood to the side an watched the EMTs give Ryan CPR. "We saw them having supper at the Watershed."

"Do you know them?" I asked Spencer.

"Ryan and Yvonne Moore. He owns the butcher shop in town," he said. "She's his fourth wife."

I'd recognized the name, but rarely went to the butcher for anything. I knew Aunt Maxi had gone there for all of her meats.

"Yeah." Patrick's brows furrowed as he nodded. "I remember him, but never see him in there when I go in there."

Patrick was a lifelong resident of Honey Springs and he did all the cooking when we were at home since I'd spent all day at the coffee house cooking for others, though I did bring a lot of leftovers home.

The bright yellow lights of the tow truck circled, lighting up the darkness. They were working on getting the truck up from the depths of the lake while the emergency workers continued to work on Ryan.

"No!" Yvonne fell to the ground, laying on Ryan.

Spencer excused himself and walked over to see what was going on. We watched as the emergency workers looked at Spencer and shook their heads.

"Oh no," I gasped bringing my hand up to my mouth, knowing Ryan Moore was dead.

RECIPES

Pumpkin Sugar Cookies-submitted by Tonya Kappes

Lemon Philly Pie- submitted by Gayle Plumb
Shanahan

Southern Pecan Bread -submitted by Tonya Kappes

Cheesecake-Stuffed Pumpkin Bread-submitted by
Susan Parham

Pumpkin Sugar Cookies

Sugar Cookies just got better with a little pumpkin! This recipe creates soft, chewy, lightly spicy glazed pumpkin sugar cookies that are perfect for Fall!

Ingredients:
1/2 cup softened butter
1/2 cup vegetable oil
1/2 cup pumpkin puree {canned pumpkin}
1 cup granulated sugar
1/2 cup powdered sugar
1/2 teaspoon vanilla
2 large eggs
4 cups all purpose flour
1/4 teaspoon baking soda
1/4 teaspoon cream of tartar
1/2 teaspoon salt
1 teaspoon cinnamon
1/2 teaspoon nutmeg

For the glaze topping:
3 cups powdered sugar
4 tablespoons water
1/4 teaspoon pumpkin pie spice

Instructions
Preheat oven to 350 degrees. Line a baking sheet with parchment paper or silicone baking mat and set aside. In a large bowl, stir butter, oil, pumpkin, sugars, vanilla and eggs together until incorporated and smooth. Slowly mix in all dry ingredients until completely incorporated. Scoop

onto prepared baking sheet using 1 1/2 tablespoon scoop and flatten to 1/2 inch thick using the bottom of a glass. If the dough is sticking to the glass, press the bottom of the glass in granulated sugar before flattening. Bake 8-9 minutes.

While cookies bake, stir all ingredients together for glaze until smooth.

Once cookies are finished baking, cool 3 minutes on baking sheet before transferring to cooling rack. Spread 1 1/2 teaspoons glaze over each warm cookie. Let glaze harden 2-3 hours before serving. OR eat them warm with lots of runny glaze.

Southern Pecan Bread

Ingredients:

1 1/2 cups light brown sugar
1/2 cup granulated sugar
1 1/4 cup butter, melted
4 eggs, lightly beaten
1 teaspoon vanilla
1/2 teaspoon kosher salt
1 1/2 cups self-rising flour
1 1/2 cups chopped pecans

Instructions:
Preheat oven to 350°F. Line a 9×13 baking dish with foil or parchment paper. Coat lightly with nonstick spray and set aside.

In the bowl of your stand mixer using the paddle attachment combine both the sugars and butter, mixing on low until combined. Add in the eggs, vanilla, and salt and turn mixer up to medium speed and mix for 1 minute until smooth.

Turn mixer to low and mix in the flour until just combined. Fold in the pecans.

Transfer mixture to your prepared pan and bake for 30-35 minutes, or until the center is just set and the edges are lightly golden.

Cool completely in the pan, and then cut into squares.

Lemon Philly Pie
(Sent in by Gayle Plumb Shanahan)

Ingredients:

3 eggs
3/4 c sugar
3/4 c lemon juice
3 t. lemon zest
12 oz. cream cheese
1/2 pt. whipping cream
Fresh raspberries

Instructions:
Beat eggs in top of double boiler until thick and fluffy.
Continue beating while gradually adding sugar, zest and lemon juice.
Cook over hot water and continue to stir constantly until lemon custard is smooth and thick.
Cool slightly and set aside.
Place cream cheese in large bowl and cream until soft and smooth.
Gradually add lemon custard to cream cheese and blend after each addition.
Place in a pre-baked pie shell and chill.
Top with raspberries and fresh sweetened whipped cream.

Cheesecake-Stuffed Pumpkin Bread
(Sent in by Susan Parham)

Ingredients Cheesecake Swirl:

One 8-ounce package cream cheese, at room temperature

1/3 cup granulated sugar

1/4 cup sour cream

1 large egg

Pumpkin Bread:

Nonstick cooking spray

1 1/3 cups all-purpose flour, plus more for dusting the pan

1/2 teaspoon baking soda

1/2 teaspoon kosher salt

3/4 cup granulated sugar

1 cup pumpkin puree

1/3 cup vegetable oil

1 teaspoon pumpkin pie spice

1 teaspoon pure vanilla extract

1 large egg

Confectioners' sugar, for dusting

Directions For the cheesecake swirl:

Position an oven rack in the bottom third of the oven and preheat the oven to 325 degrees
F.

Combine the cream cheese, granulated sugar, sour cream and egg in a large bowl and beat
with a mixer until well combined; set aside.

For the pumpkin bread:

Generously spray a 9-by-5-inch loaf pan with nonstick spray and dust with flour.

Whisk together the flour, baking soda and salt in a medium bowl and set aside.

Whisk together the granulated sugar and pumpkin puree in a large bowl, then whisk in the oil, pumpkin pie spice, vanilla and egg.

Whisk in the flour mixture until just combined.

Reserve 1 cup of the pumpkin batter.

Spread the remaining batter in the bottom of the prepared loaf pan.

Spoon the cream cheese mixture over the pumpkin batter, then put the reserved cup pumpkin batter in a line down the center of the pan.

Insert the tip of a paring knife into the batter and drag it through and up to swirl 5 to 6 times.

Bake until the top is cracked and a cake tester inserted in the center comes out clean, 1 hour 15 minutes to 1 hour 20 minutes.

Cool on a wire rack for 30 minutes, then carefully invert onto a platter or cake stand and flip upright.

Let cool completely, at least 1 1/2 hours.

Dust with confectioners' sugar and serve.

Also by Tonya Kappes

A CHARMING MISFORTUNE

A Camper and Criminals Cozy Mystery

BEACHES, BUNGALOWS, & BURGLARIES

DESERTS, DRIVERS, & DERELICTS

FORESTS, FISHING, & FORGERY

CHRISTMAS, CRIMINALS, & CAMPERS

MOTORHOMES, MAPS, & MURDER

CANYONS, CARAVANS, & CADAVERS

HITCHES, HIDEOUTS, & HOMICIDE

ASSAILANTS, ASPHALT, & ALIBIS

VALLEYS, VEHICLES & VICTIMS

A Southern Cake Baker Series

(under the pen name of Maymee Bell)

CAKE AND PUNISHMENT

BATTER OFF DEAD

A Ghostly Southern Mystery Series

A GHOSTLY UNDERTAKING

A GHOSTLY GRAVE

A GHOSTLY DEMISE

A GHOSTLY MURDER

A GHOSTLY REUNION

A GHOSTLY MORTALITY

A GHOSTLY SECRET

A GHOSTLY SUSPECT

Killer Coffee Mystery Series

SCENE OF THE GRIND

MOCHA AND MURDER

FRESHLY GROUND MURDER

COLD BLOODED BREW

DECAFFEINATED SCANDAL

A KILLER LATTE

HOLIDAY ROAST MORTEM

MAIL CARRIER COZY MYSTERY

STAMPED OUT

ADDRESSED FOR MURDER

Kenni Lowry Mystery Series

FIXIN' TO DIE

SOUTHERN FRIED

AX TO GRIND

SIX FEET UNDER

DEAD AS A DOORNAIL

TANGLED UP IN TINSEL

DIGGIN' UP DIRT

Spies and Spells Mystery Series

SPIES AND SPELLS

BETTING OFF DEAD

GET WITCH or DIE TRYING

A Laurel London Mystery Series

CHECKERED CRIME

CHECKERED PAST

CHECKERED THIEF

A Divorced Diva Beading Mystery Series

A BEAD OF DOUBT SHORT STORY

STRUNG OUT TO DIE

CRIMPED TO DEATH

Olivia Davis Paranormal Mystery Series

SPLITSVILLE.COM

COLOR ME LOVE (novella)

COLOR ME A CRIME

About the Author

Tonya has written over 60 novels and four novellas, all of which have graced numerous bestseller lists, including the USA Today. *Best known for stories charged with emotion and humor and filled with flawed characters, her novels have garnered reader praise and glowing critical reviews. She lives with her husband and a very spoiled rescue cat named Ro. Tonya grew up in the small southern Kentucky town of Nicholasville. Now that her four boys are grown men, Tonya writes full-time.*

Visit Tonya:

I host weekly giveaways, contests, recipes and fun on my weekly Tuesday Coffee Chat with Tonya~ sign up here >>>

https://landing.mailerlite.com/webforms/landing/r9x5u8

Tonya Kappes Online Cozy Krew Book Group

https://www.facebook.com/groups/208579765929709/

Webpage

http://www.tonyakappes.com/

Facebook at Author Tonya Kappes,

https://www.facebook.com/authortonyakappes

Goodreads

https://www.goodreads.com/author/show/4423580.Tonya_
Kappes

Twitter

https://twitter.com/tonyakappes11

Pinterest

https://www.pinterest.com/tonyakappes/

For weekly updates and contests, sign up for Coffee Chat
with Tonya newsletter via her website or Facebook.

Copyright

Made in the USA
Monee, IL
21 June 2020